STUNTBOY,
IN-BETWEEN TIME

by **Jason Reynolds**
drawings by **Raúl the Third**

(LIVE IN FRONT OF A STUDIO AUDIENCE)

A CAITLYN DLOUHY BOOK
Atheneum Books for Young Readers
NEW YORK LONDON TORONTO SYDNEY NEW DELHI

ATHENEUM BOOKS FOR YOUNG READERS

An imprint of Simon & Schuster Children's Publishing Division

1230 Avenue of the Americas, New York, New York 10020

For information about special discounts for bulk purchases, please contact Simon & Schuster Special Sales at 1-866-506-1949 or business@simonandschuster.com.

The Simon & Schuster Speakers Bureau can bring authors to your live event. For more information or to book an event, contact the Simon & Schuster Speakers Bureau at 1-866-248-3049 or visit our website at www.simonspeakers.com.

The text for this book was set in Kabouter.

The illustrations for this book were rendered digitally.

Manufactured in China

0423 SCP

First Edition

2 4 6 8 10 9 7 5 3 1

CIP data for this book is available from the Library of Congress.

ISBN 9781534418226

ISBN 9781534418240 (ebook)

For my older brother, Allen, and my younger brother, Christian, for being incredible examples of kindness. Even though Allen beat me up a lot when we were young
—Jason

For my two brothers, Danny and Ruben Gonzalez, who I ran wild with at Village Two apartments
—Raúl

PREVIOUSLY, ON STUNTBOY, IN THE MEANTIME:

Portico Reeves lives in the biggest building on the block. Skylight Gardens. And even though Skylight Gardens doesn't have any skylights, or gardens, it's the best place in the world to Portico.

Only problem is, sometimes, when life gets uncomfortable, everything in his body gets uncomfortable too. He calls this . . . *the frets.*

The only person who ever seems to get Portico un-fretted is his best friend, Zola Brawner. They've been best friends for, hmm . . . let's see . . . 216 days.

The person who used to cause a lot of the frets is a boy named Herbert Singletary.

Herbert Singletary used to be **THE WORST.**
Now . . . not so much. Now he hangs out with
Portico and Zola. Weird.

Portico, with the help of Zola,
became STUNTBOY.
Back in the Mean Time.

Stuntboy's superpower is to do all the hard stunts so the heroes don't have to do any. You know, the big jumps, and high dives, and **bangs!** and **crashes!** and **ka-pows!**

Stuntboy knows how to do, like, a **million** stunts. At least. **And he's saved a gazillion people.** At most.

But no stunt—

not the Potato Bug, or the Zamarama Zigzag, or even the Plaster Blaster—could save his parents from . . .

from . . .

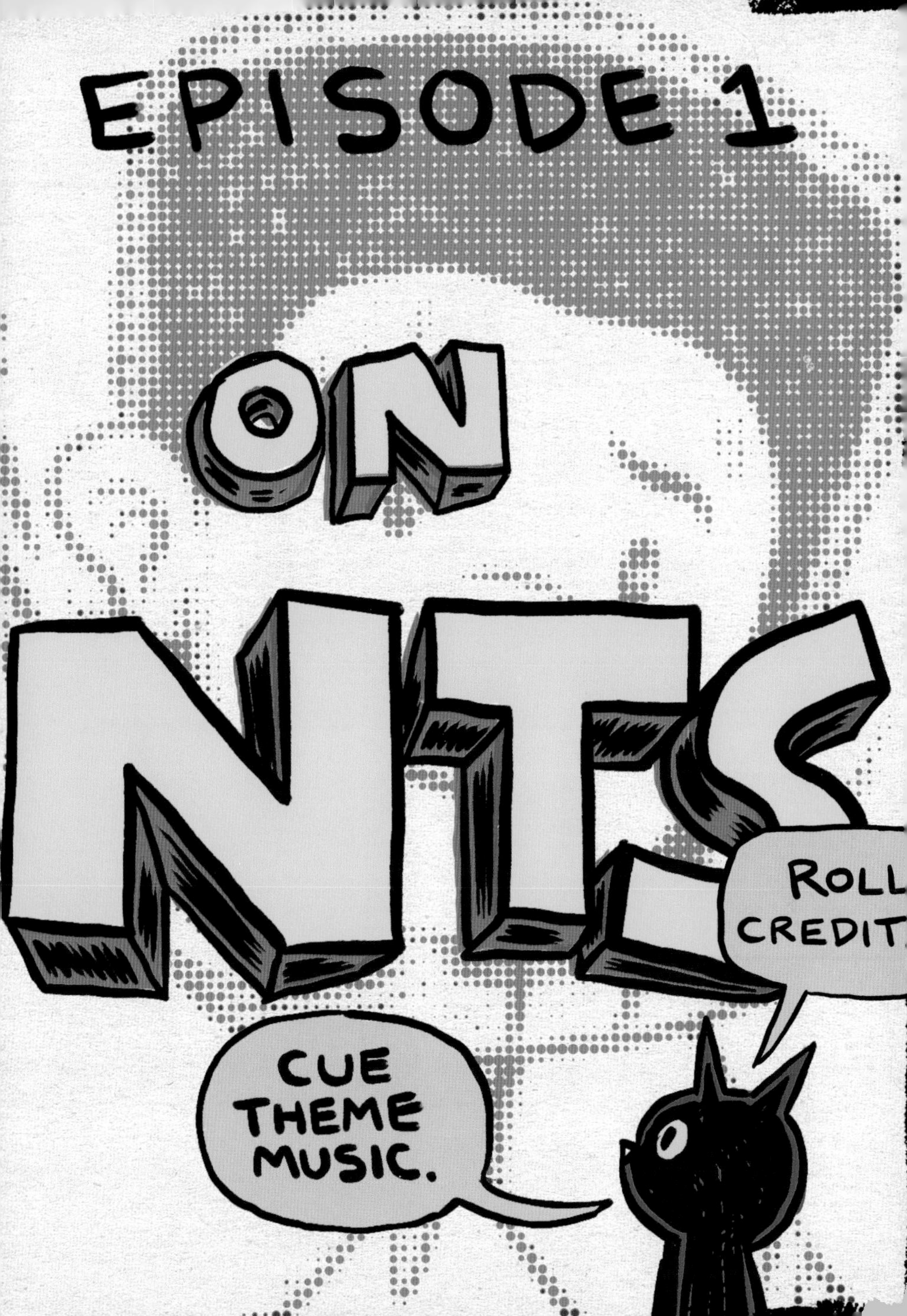
EPISODE 1
ON
NITS
ROLL
CREDIT
CUE THEME MUSIC.

But can we use the harp?

What do you mean
"we don't have a harp"?
Of course we do!

No? Not anymore?
Who could just walk out
of here with a gigantic harp
without anyone seeing?

You know what . . . never mind.

Except, tell me, how are we supposed
to make dream sounds with no harp?
I guess we'll just have to make
blings, **blangs**, and **blongs**
with our mouths, huh?
Not the same, but . . .
it'll have to do.

And a **one**, and a **two**, and a . . .

WeLLLlllLcoMe to
STUNtboy YYyy
in-BeTWEeeeen Time!!!

REINTRODUCING THE ONE AND ONLY . . .

Stuntboy. He's the best superhero most people have never heard of. But **you've** heard of him because, well, **you're** smart, and trustworthy, and keep your eyes on all the secret superheroes, which happens to be your secret superpower but, hey, this story ain't about you.

This story's about Stuntboy.

And also, it's about what you know about Stuntboy. Like how he **loves television and drawing** (way more than books). Or how he lives on the fourth floor in Skylight Gardens, the big castle with the glassiest glass and the brickiest bricks on Earth.

At least he **used** to. I mean, he still lives in the castle but now he lives on the fifth floor.

And the third floor.

And now you're thinking two things: **How does he have two apartments in the castle? His superpower must be being in two places at once.** Well, he wishes. But no. Your second thought is, **Or he must be rich!** Yeah, that's what Portico thought too. At first. He thought Skylight Gardens was going to be renamed "The Portico Palace." Or, "The Reeves Resort." But, turns out, that's not true either. The real reason he now lives in two apartments is because his parents . . . um . . . his parents, they, uh . . . they . . .

(JUST SAY IT ALREADY!)

Portico's parents became X's. Yeah . . . hard. And hard to pronounce. I mean, because it's basically just made of two I's, an X should make the sound of I. But big. A big loud I. But maybe because the two I's cross, they jumble up the sound and that makes everything hard. So now X sounds like . . . *ecks*, or just *ks*, or *shhh*, or, *zz*. It's the only real mixed-up letter, and mixed-up letters sometimes do mixed-up things. Like . . .

(JUST SAY IT ALREADY!)

. . . like, break up. And become two separate I's again. Which caused Portico to **break down**. And cry **his eyes out**.

It had only been about six days since the big split, and on the seventh day, Portico was supposed to spend the night at his father's apartment. Apartment 3C.

For the first time.

This should've been great news. But to Portico, spending the night at his father's place meant accepting the fact that his father's place was . . . real, which meant his mother and father's breakup was . . . **real**, which meant the upside-downing of his family was . . . **real**, and that was . . . **real** hard. Normally, he would've been excited to spend the weekend doing father-son things, but he'd never had to do that without the day ending with his parents doing mom-dad things. Now his mom and dad were busy doing **we don't like each other** things, which to Portico was just a whole bunch of **this don't make sense** things, which made his body do **bumble jumble rumble** things.

IN CASE YOU FORGOT

Frets (FRETS!) are when Portico's insides became a jigsaw puzzle put together all wrong. And tonight, the night before his first weekend with his dad, the frets had decided to keep him awake. Puzzling. His inside-things running around each floor of his body. His Grunge Sponge and his Gas Tank were having a dance contest like the one he and Zola had at Zola's birthday party a few weeks before. His Squigglies and Beaner Cleaner were bouncing off the walls acting out their favorite TV shows. (Had they ever heard of *Super Space Warriors*? Of course they had! They literally live inside Portico!)

Anyway, the point is, once Portico finally fell asleep, the frets showed up there, too. In his dreams.

UPPSY-DOWNSY

In this dream, Portico was on the fourth floor outside his old apartment, but strangely, the door was bolted shut. That didn't stop him from trying to open it. As he yanked and yanked on the door, he heard his father calling him.

"Portico!" His father's voice echoed throughout the building.

Portico ran to the stairwell to get a better listen.

"Portico! Portico!" His father's voice was now louder.

PORTICO!

Portico started down the stairs, but after he jumped down one flight (which should've landed him on the third floor) he realized something was wrong. Because instead, he was on the fifth floor.

Weird, he thought. But the weirdness of it all didn't stop him from trying to find his father—because **that** would be weird—so he trotted down the next staircase. To his surprise (a second surprise!) he was now on the sixth floor. Confused and frustrated, Portico stormed down flight after flight after flight—more flights than actually exist in Skylight Gardens—but the numbers kept going up, until finally he heard his mother's voice.

"Portico!" she cried out from below him.

Portico turned around and headed back up the steps—flight after flight—but this time, though he was going up, the floor numbers were going down. And up and up he went. And down and down the numbers went.

Up was down.

Down was up.

And no one was anywhere to be found.

"Portico!" his mother called, again. "Up, Portico! Up!"

DAD-URDAY

Portico's mother was shaking him awake.

Portico opened his eyes even though it felt like he'd just closed them. His mother kissed him on the forehead.

"Wake up, baby," she said. "Time for me to go."

"Where you going?" Portico gurgled.

"I told you last night. Mrs. Brawner invited me to a

meditation retreat. I figured it might be nice for me to try something new."

"Oh, that's good," Portico replied, only half awake. If he had been more awake, maybe he would've said that all anyone in their family seemed to be doing were new things. Mom lived in a new place, which meant Portico lived in a new place. Dad lived in a new place, which meant, after tonight, Portico lived in a(nother) new place. And Gran Gran lived with Dad, so she was also in a new place. And the cat, A New Name Every Day . . . well, the cat pretty much did whatever it wanted. "You want some advice?"

"I'd love some, especially from you," his mother said, her face somewhere between rested and wrestling, which is how it's looked since the big split.

Portico sat up, because you can't give advice lying down.

"Okay. So, when it comes to meditation'ing, all you have to remember is to make yourself a pretzel and take a bunch of deep breaths through your toes." Portico's mother pretended to write this down with an invisible pen on an invisible piece of paper.

"Pretzel . . . toes . . . got it. Anything else?"

"Well, you might wanna focus more on your thumb toes because your pinky toes have corns, and corn and pretzels don't really go that good together," Portico advised.

"Wow . . . okay. I'll be sure to keep that in mind. You just make sure to go down to your father's apartment. And when you get there, promise me there will be no pretzels involved. No twists, no knots, and no salt between you two, understand?"

Portico had no idea what his mother was talking about. "Not really?"

"I just mean, promise me you'll try to enjoy yourself."

That seemed like a strange thing to promise because Portico's father was always enjoyable. Enjoyable could've been his father's first name. It wasn't. It was Marvin, which might mean enjoyable in another language. Like an alien language. But that would make Portico's father part alien. Which would make Portico part alien. Which would explain why Portico has eleven toes.

Just kidding. He has twelve, like everyone else.

Just kidding, again. Maybe.

Anyway, the point is, Portico's father was usually so enjoyable his name could've been Enjoyable Reeves.

Here's why: First of all, Portico's dad had the **coolest job in the world**. Honestly. Like, people always want to be the president, but it doesn't seem like the president can have friends. And having no friends doesn't seem enjoyable at all, which means being the president can't be all that fun.

School teacher seems cool, because they get summer break, but it seems pretty risky to teach because what if you get a class full of Herbert Singletaries, back when he was still the Worst? I mean, if you get a class of Zolas, teaching would be awesome, but even Portico knew Zola was the only Zola. So . . . yeah, being a teacher was a gamble. Honestly, other than Ice Cream Truck Driver, and Ice Cream Flavor Taster (Tester? Taster? Both?), or Potato Chip Cruncher Muncher, or . . . I mean . . . Super Space Warrior, there was no better job than the one Portico's father had:

Trash man.

WHY IT'S COOL to be a TRASHMAN!

1. You get to ride and feed the trash monster, which, if we're being honest, is the coolest thing anyone could ever do.

2. You get an excuse to stink without a grown-up telling you to take a bath. Stink is just part of the job.

3. You find cool stuff. One person's trash is another person's . . . future trash. But everything is cool when it's new. Even when it's old. Except grown-ups. Unless they're trash men. Or trash women. Trash people. Who aren't trash . . . people.

Though Portico was **nervous** about staying at his father's place, one thing he was **excited** about was the possibility that **this might be the weekend his dad would let him come on the garbage truck.** His mother had bagged up lots of things from their old apartment. Things that weren't split up in the split-up. Like bath mats and soap dishes and a cracked coffee pot and old remote controls and flower pots and paper cups and paper plates and paper clips and paper paper. Just . . . stuff. And Portico was supposed to take it all down to the trash chute that went down to the big trash trough that the garbage monsters ate from. But instead of dumping the bag, Portico saved it. It would be much cooler to go through it with his father first, just in case he wanted any of it.

BREAKFAST OF SUPERHEROES

Oatmeal is healthy. And it tastes like it, right? I mean, who thought it was a good idea to have an oat . . . meal? Like, a whole meal of just oats. Seriously, if we didn't know oats could be eaten, we would just assume they were dirt. Or bird food, but not even, because birds eat seeds and stuff. Unless you live in Skylight Gardens, where birds eat leftover pizza and breakfast sandwiches, all better options than oatmeal. So instead of eating oatmeal, which is what Portico's mother made him for breakfast, Portico decided to take every kind of cereal in the cabinet—Sugar Circles, Sugar Flakes, Sugar Crispies, Sugar Sugars—and pour them all into the same bowl as the oatmeal. Then he bathed them in chocolate milk. After that, he let it all soak in the bowl until it got soggy, which basically made it . . . ahem . . . sorta . . . kinda . . . oatmeal! But delicious!

Portico was washing his bowl when there was a knock at the door. It was one of his favorite people—the strawberry-candy dealer, the purple-hair princess, the classy couch potato, the queen of the resting eyes—Gran Gran!

"Helloooo," Gran Gran sang, kissing Portico's face.

"How was Las Vegas?" Portico's mother asked. Gran Gran and Portico's father had gone on vacation for the week. Not sure if you know anything about Las Vegas, but it's basically like hanging out in a giant pinball machine in the middle of the desert. Dad was trying something new too.

"Fantastic. Seven-Seven-Seven!" Grandma bragged.

"What's that mean?" Portico asked.

"That's the lucky number. Means I hit the jackpot!"

"What?! For how much?" Portico's mother asked, surprised.

"Seven dollars and sixty-five cents!" Gran Gran was totally pleased with herself. She dug through her purse. "And . . . I used it to buy this!" Gran Gran pulled out a refrigerator magnet from her bag. She handed it to Portico. "For you."

WHAT MAGNETS ARE FOR:

1. To stick a list of chores your mom wants you to do to the refrigerator.
2. To help you remember the name and address of your doctor's office.
3. To help with reading and writing. Magnetic letters are the best!
4. To remember a vacation someone else went on.
5. To make a refrigerator pretty.
6. To make a house a home.

"Thanks, Gran Gran," Portico said, admiring the souvenir before slipping it into his pocket because it was the first time he'd ever owned a magnet, and he just wasn't ready to share it with his mom by adding it to her big collection stuck to the fridge. "Did Dad hit the jackpot too?" He was excited by the possibility.

"Nope!" Gran Gran said plainly before lining herself up along Mom's new couch, preparing herself for a flop down on its cushions.

Once flopped, she leaned back, leaned forward, bounced up and down.

"What you think?" Portico's mother asked.

"Meh. It ain't been tenderized yet. So it's still a sofa. But it'll be a couch eventually."

"Gran Gran, what you doing here?" Portico asked.

"Oh, how I've missed you!" Gran Gran said, hugging A New Name Every Day. "And you, too, Portico. Can't a grandma come see her grandson?"

"I didn't mean it like that. I just meant I'm not gonna be **here** because I gotta go stay at Dad's. And since that's where you live now too, I thought I'd just see you when I got there."

"I know. But I figured I'd stay **here** tonight. That way I can give your father a chance to rest today—losing is exhausting—and plus, you two can have some quality time together.

"Oh, Dad's resting? I should probably just catch him another time."

"No, no, he's never too tired for you," Gran Gran assured him. "Also, I need to talk your mom into trimming the hair on my face. Lashes, brows, 'stache, and these few growing outta here." Gran Gran pinched and plucked her chin hair.

"Can't today, Gran Gran," Portico's mother said, spritzing herself with perfume. "I'm on my way out."

Where you going?

"To learn how to meditate."

"To learn how to **what?**"

"How to meditate. How to find my center."

Gran Gran flashed a funny face at Portico.

"Come here, grandson, let me show your mother how to find her center."

Portico came closer. Sat on the couch. Gran Gran poked his stomach.

"See? The center's right here!" Gran Gran said, tickling Portico. He laughed and laughed and snorted and even . . . well . . .

Commercial Break

BRAP!

This commercial is brought to you by

THINGS NOT TO SAY THAT YOU'LL ALWAYS WANT TO SAY AND SO . . . YOU SHOULD SAY THEM:

1. . . . farted.

2. Also known as **pooted.**

3. Also known as **tooted.**

4. Should be known as **blew a tire.**

5. Or even better, **played a little funky trumpet.**

Now back to your regularly scheduled program.

After Portico's mom left, and Gran Gran continued to work out her relationship with the new sofa, Portico did what he always did this time of the morning. Practiced his stunts. Just part of his daily routine. Wake up, wash up, eat up, then trip, flip, and slip up. And with Gran Gran there it seemed especially special. Extra specially. Because it felt like old times.

Note: Old times was a week ago.

Portico had thought up a bunch of new stunts. He and A New Name Every Day tried them out. First, the **Laptop Juice Spill**, which is when you pretend to be a laptop with juice spilled on it, which means you just go winky-wonky and blink your eyes real fast.

LAPTOP JUICE SPILL

NEW STUNTS

HIPPO HIPPITY HOP OVER

Then, the **Hippo Hippity Hop Over**, which is when you get down on all fours and jump. Well, it's really more of a pounce, but you always land on all fours, too. It's a tough one. Only for professionals.

TOWER OF FLOWER

Then, there's the **Tower of Sour**, which is when you stand still and suck your cheeks in like a fish. Not to be confused with the **Tower of Flower**, which is when you stand still and pluck your hair out, strand after strand (ouch!).

Not to be confused with the **Tower of Flour** which Portico has only done once and got in so much trouble with his mom that he promised to never do it again, but . . . it involves flour being blown everywhere. Not to be confused with the Unhealthy Oatmeal, which Portico had just made up at breakfast.

TOWER OF FLOUR

"Woo!" Gran Gran howled. "Hey, you think you can maybe teach me some of these?"

"Uh . . . I don't know. They're pretty dangerous," Portico explained.

"Oh, you gotta be a superhero to do stuff like this, huh?" Gran Gran said, and Portico immediately stood still. Super still. Steel still. Did Gran Gran know he was Stuntboy?! She couldn't have. But grandmas know stuff. Like when you haven't taken a bath. Or how chicken mixed with noodles and salty water makes feeling sick go away.

"I don't know," Portico said, evasively.

"Okay. Well, can I at least have a superhero name? If I were a superhero, which I kinda am, what would my name be?" She rubbed her chin. Portico rubbed his butt. He'd landed on it pretty hard when he spilled over doing the Laptop Juice Spill.

"You don't need one." Portico replied skeptically. **Why was she asking about superhero stuff?**

"Do Zola got one? That little girl deserves a superhero name."

"She don't need one either."

"And why is that?" Gran Gran's eyes slivered. Her head tilted. She did not like that answer.

"Because, Gran Gran, her name is Zola. Zola. No superhero name is better than Zola."

Grandma un-slivered her eyes, straightened her head, nodded. "Good point. What about that other one?"

"Who, Herbert?"

"Uh-huh."

Portico hadn't ever thought about Herbert Singletary as a potential superhero. Mainly because he had been Portico's **supervillain** for so long. But now that they were friends, maybe Herbert **should** have one. He was a Super's son, after all. And he had a secret base, which was the boiler room, and he used to be the leader of the weenagers, which meant he was a leader. And the best superheroes are definitely leaders.

"Not yet," Portico said, now thinking about it. Herbert Singletary the Superhero wasn't good enough. Plus, Portico didn't even know what Herbert's superpowers were, and that had to be figured out before there could be a name. So much to consider.

Stunt practice went on, and Gran Gran went on clapping and cheering until she clapped and cheered herself to sleep, which to most people would've been weird because it was morning, but Gran Gran didn't care if it was morning, noon, or night. When her eyes needed a timeout, they always took it.

ON HIS WAY

Portico, now fully prepared for whatever the day might bring, dragged the trash bag out of his new fifth-floor apartment. But instead of turning left and heading toward the trash chute, he went to the right. Toward the elevator. This trash was for father-son time. Quality time. Making it quality trash.

Plus it was too heavy to take the stairs.

He lugged the bag past the door of one of his new neighbors, Baby Sis Brown, whose name sounds young, but she wasn't. She was an older lady who wore ten watches, each set to a different time. She even

had a clock on the outside of her apartment door and was setting it as Portico tramped by.

"Doing okay, Ms. Brown?" Portico asked.

"Hey, Portico. Just setting my clock back twenty minutes."

"Why?"

WEE OOO WEE OOO!!!!

"Because twenty minutes ago, I heard a joke that made me laugh harder than I've laughed in years. Seems like a good time to revisit, you know?"

Portico didn't quite understand, but . . . he also kinda did. There were moments he wished he could revisit too. Like when his mom and dad took him on a roller coaster for the first time and his dad screamed like a police siren. Or all the Friday night movies they'd watch together, and how every week someone got to make the popcorn, which was fun because everyone had their own popcorn recipes.

His dad liked to add butter and garlic powder.

His mom liked to add chili powder and a little sugar.

And Portico . . . well, he put on **everything**.

He wished he could go back to all that. But he couldn't. No clock told time good enough to tell **that** time in Portico's life to come back. The hours of **ours**.

When the elevator doors opened, standing there was Ms. Rosedale, humming at the top of her lungs. Do you have any idea how annoying loud humming is? Let's just say Portico was happy he didn't have too many floors to go, because if Ms. Rosedale was in the elevator, Portico knew she'd already hit every button and he'd have to suffer through all that humming. Because she **always** hit every single button. And never hit a single note.

"Hi, Ms. Rosedale."

"Who's that?" Ms. Rosedale asked, squinting at Portico.

"It's me, Portico."

"What's that?"

"I said, it's me, Portico!"

"I heard you, but what's **that**?" Ms. Rosedale pointed at the trash bag.

"Oh, it's for my dad."

"Wow, things sure have changed. When I was young, a gift was a gift. Came wrapped in a box with a bow. Now they just come in trash bags." Ms. Rosedale shook her head. "But I know you going through a tough time right now with your parents breaking up, so . . ." she trailed off.

And before Portico could respond, before he could ask Ms. Rosedale how she even knew about his parents' divorce, she began humming again.

BEST THING TO HAPPEN ON AN ELEVATOR:

Music. Not coming from a person **on** the elevator, but the music made **for** the elevator. Nothing like the sweet sounds of elevator music. It makes it seem like every elevator is leading you right to a beach. But in Skylight Gardens, there was no music. Unless you count people like Ms. Rosedale, or the sound of the old elevator trying its best to work, which I guess could be considered "rock and roll."

WORST THING TO HAPPEN ON AN ELEVATOR:

Getting stuck.

WHAT HAPPENED TO PORTICO ON THE ELEVATOR ON HIS WAY TO HIS FATHER'S APARTMENT:

Exactly that. The elevator got stuck. Which meant
Portico . . . GOT STUCK!

Which meant . . .

Portico's heart split in half, one half jumping into his throat,
the other half falling into his belly, each half of this organ
becoming a drum, beating at different paces. The one in
the throat going **boom-de-boomboom boom-de-
boomboom** and the one in the belly going **bop-bip-
thumpalump bop-bip-thumpalump.**

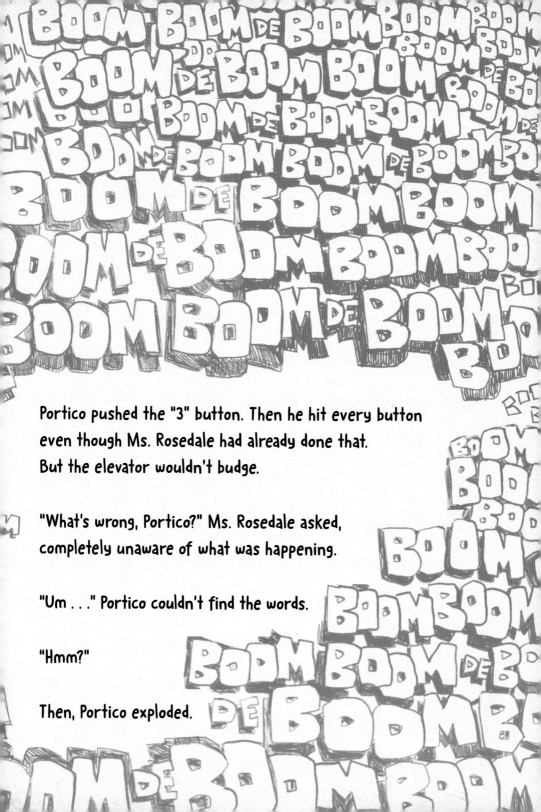

Portico pushed the "3" button. Then he hit every button
even though Ms. Rosedale had already done that.
But the elevator wouldn't budge.

"What's wrong, Portico?" Ms. Rosedale asked,
completely unaware of what was happening.

"Um . . ." Portico couldn't find the words.

"Hmm?"

Then, Portico exploded.

Ms. Rosedale I don't know how to tell you this so I'm just gonna say it and I have no clue how you're gonna react and that scares me because if something bad happens to you while we're in here I'm not sure I know how to fix you or help you or anything like that but my Gran Gran has been teaching me CPR since I was five but I don't remember everything but I do remember something called hime lick but I don't really want to lick your himes because I don't know what himes are but they sound like they have something to do with feet and I remember this other thing that has to do with punching the stomach but I think it would be rude to punch you in the stomach and I don't think I could do that or maybe that's the hime lick and I just don't remember because I just can't remember anything right now except for that one scene in Episode 31 of *Super Space Warriors* when Mater and Pater got stuck in the *Sunjet* and they just kept hitting the open-door button over and over and over and over again until the whole *Sunjet* started shaking and smoking and making *ant! ant! ant!* sounds until finally there was . . .

AN EXPLOSION OF GREAT MAGNITUDE!

Oh, that's nice.

"Ms. Rosedale—THE ELEVATOR IS STUCK!"

It seemed to take a second for the words to get into Ms. Rosedale's brain. But when they did, well . . .

"AHHHHHHHHHHHHHHHHHHHHHHHHHH!"
Ms. Rosedale screamed.

"AHHHHHHHHHHH!" Portico screamed.

AHHHHHHHHHHHH!!

SEE YA LATER, ELEVATOR!

Portico, what are we gonna do?

Portico didn't have an answer.

Ms. Rosedale's face started to look sick. All the color drained from it, and her eyes had gone wonky. Portico could only think of one thing—Ms. Rosedale needed . . . STUNTBOY!

Stuntboy yelled, spinning and spinning and spinning and spinning and spinning, before getting so dizzy that he literally had no choice but to flop down on his butt. Right on the already-sore spot.

BUT STUNTBOY WASN'T DONE YET. HE HAD MORE.

Portico lay flat on his back and began kicking his legs up and down, banging his heels on the elevator floor. This was his last resort. A special stunt, only meant for real emergencies.

And before Ms. Rosedale could say anything else, the elevator rumbled, jerked, and knocked back as if responding to Portico's feet. Then its doors opened.

They'd only gone one floor, and were now on the fourth. Ms. Rosedale thanked Portico and ran . . . no, SPRINTED from the elevator. Portico had never seen her run. No one had. She could barely see, but it didn't matter to her if she ran into a wall as long as it wasn't an elevator wall. And as Portico slowly got to his feet, he noticed his friends, Zola and Herbert Singletary the Okay, standing in the hallway and staring into the open doors of the still shuddering elevator.

"Yeah." Portico was trying to catch his breath. "I am now," he said, half crawling out of the elevator.

episode
2

BUTTER'S NEVER BEEN SO BAD

Roll credits. Cue theme music. Wait, cut! Cut!

What's that? What, you don't hear it? Sounds like . . .

Is that construction? That's construction, isn't it?
A jackhammer? Are they jackhammering right outside?
And is that a blow torch? What in the world are they
torching? Maybe they're building a new set. I mean, we sure
could use an elevator.

They picked a fine time to do this, but whatever.
The show must go on.

And a one, and a two,
and . . .

WelLLLIIILcoMe to
STUNtboyYYyy in-betwEen
Time!

ZAP!

JACK!
JACK!
JACK!
JACK!

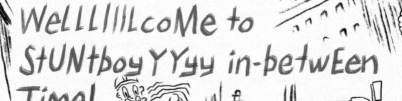

Add a little Pepper

By the time Portico had dragged his bag of trash to where Zola and Herbert were standing, his frets had started to settle.

"You okay, bro?" Herbert asked. He and Portico had been friends for thirteen days, which is more than enough time to be able to read a friend's mind. Not to mention, face. I mean, Portico and Zola had been best best friends for thirteen days by their thirteenth day of knowing each other. With Herbert it would take a little more time to be best best friends since he spent at least 483 days as the worst worst. But still, Herbert could see Portico was fretting.

"Just got stuck in the elevator," Portico said, trying to get his heart to go from bang to beat again.

"Yikes. I better tell my stepdad it's broken."

"I'm sure Soup already knows. Ms. Rosedale's probably on the phone with him right now."

"What's with the bag?" Zola asked.

"It's trash."

"You know there's a chute on every floor, right?" Zola replied.

"Of course I know that," Portico snapped. "But I'm taking this down to my dad's. For father-son time."

Herbert said, "Usually father-son time is . . . playing catch, or—"

Zola pushed the door to her place open. "This better be good," she said to Herbert.

"You coming in, or you going to your dad's right now?" she said to Portico.

"Welllll . . ." Portico knew, in the front of his mind, that he was supposed to be on his way. But in the back of his mind, way back there in the knuckle part of his head, he knew he didn't want to. Because to get one step closer to his dad's apartment meant he was one step closer to his parents' **apart**-ment.

"Come on," Herbert egged. Portico pretended to think about it.

"Maybe just for like . . . sixteen minutes," Portico said. "But only if I can bring my trash."

"I . . . guess," Zola said.

"Thanks," Portico said. "Just gonna wait for Soup to fix the elevator, which should only take him about sixteen minutes because he's a Super. Then I gotta jet."

"How's the two-apartment thing going, anyway?" Herbert asked as Portico heaved his bag into Zola's living room.

"Weird. A new place, less voices in the house, more voices in my head. Just . . . weird. Even being on a different floor is strange. Smells funny without Mama Gloria's cooking stinkin' up everything." He plopped down on one of the lawn chairs in Zola's living room.

"Your dad home?" Herbert asked Zola, ready to tell them the thing he'd come to tell them. A special secret.

"Nah. He's down at Mr. Hall's place," Zola said. Mr. Hall was the Skylight Gardens Chess Champion forty years in a row. People used to call him the king of chess, but he didn't like that, because the queen is the most powerful piece on the board. So he calls himself the queen of chess. "My dad's trying to convince him to buy lawn chairs so he can at least relax while kicking everybody's butt. Dad's even calling them 'pawn chairs.'" Zola rolled her eyes. Turned to Portico. "And you know my mom's with your mom at some kind of meditation retreat."

"Yeah. My mom's gonna be **mad** when she finds out she's gonna have to run with her eyes closed," Portico said.

"Why would they be running with their eyes closed?" Zola was perplexed.

Portico threw his arms up. "That's what I wanna know! I mean, I know what 'meditation' means. And 'retreat' means to run. I've seen them do it all the time on *Super Space Warriors*. So . . ."

"Nope. I mean, yes, but . . . no, no, no," Zola said, shaking her head. "A retreat is also like an event."

"Tell me about it!" Portico said, missing the point.

"I mean, it's less like a run-away, and more like a . . . **get**away," Zola explained.

Suddenly, Portico heard the sound of the toilet flushing.

"I thought you said your dad wasn't home," Herbert said, now tucking his secret back under his tongue.

"He's not. That's my—"

"Here's your Good Morning Warning!" A man came blasting into the living room.

The man screamed. Hollered. Howled. Good Morning had
never been so loud. Portico and Herbert were stunned.
Zola . . . not so much.

"Portico, Herbert, this is Grandpa Pepper," Zola said, looking
a little embarrassed.

Grandpa Pepper had a face like a baby if a baby had a face
like an old man. He didn't have a single strand of hair on his
cheeks, and the hair on top of his head had a courtyard right
in the middle of it. He wore his pants pulled up so high that
it made his legs look too long, and the rest of him too short.
He wore funky glasses, and even funkier jewelry. He even
had some of his nails painted.

"Portico?" Grandpa Pepper asked, confirming Portico's name.

"Yes sir."

"Okay, okay! Nice to meet you,
Porchie! Lay your lines
on mine!" Grandpa
Pepper held his
hand out.

Portico was confused for a few reasons. One reason was he had no idea who Porchie was, especially since he'd just confirmed his name was Portico. And the second reason was that Portico didn't have any lines. At least he didn't think he did. Why would he have lines? What kind of lines? Lines where?

Zola came to Portico's rescue. As usual.

"He means the lines in your hand," she said, showing Portico the creases in his palm. "He's just asking you for a handshake."

Portico, relieved, shook Grandpa Pepper's hand.

"Nice to meet ya, Porchie," Grandpa Pepper said, shaking Portico's hand.

"Portico."

"Right, Porchie."

"His name's Portico, Grandpa," Zola said.

"I know! But a portico is a porch. A beautiful porch with pillars. Ain't you a porch with pillars, son?"

"Um . . ." Portico didn't know what to say. He didn't know that was what his name meant, and he hadn't considered himself a porch. Plus he didn't have a lot of experience with porches because he lived in a castle. He was probably more of a lobby. Or maybe even an elevator, going up and down until getting stuck.

"You too, Air Bear!" Grandpa Pepper now said to Herbert. "Put your lines on mine."

"Who's Air Bear?" It was now Herbert's turn to shake Grandpa Pepper's hand, but Herbert wasn't so sure he wanted to.

"Who's Air Bear? You Air Bear, Air Bear!"

"But my name's Herbert."

"Not in France!"

"Huh?"

"Just shake his hand," Zola hissed. Herbert followed Zola's instructions and shook Grandpa Pepper's hand, and then Grandpa Pepper explained he'd come to see Zola and hang around while her mother was off meditation'ing with Portico's mom.

Zola turned the TV on and pulled out all her pencils, crayons, and markers, as well as a bunch of paper. *Super Space Warriors* was just starting—a new episode from the new season featuring two new Warrior Trainees, Frater and Soror.

Portico, Zola, and Herbert tried drawing along with the show because, in case you forgot, drawing is cool. Definitely cooler than books. But not cooler than TV. But still pretty cool. But this time, the drawing session was a little different because Grandpa Pepper was there. And he had soooooo much to say.

"Oh, Portico, I love that color you're using on Mater's helmet. What do you call it?" Grandpa Pepper asked.

Portico was immediately concerned that maybe Grandpa Pepper was color blind. He'd heard about people who couldn't see color.

"Um . . . it's . . . just red," Portico said, shrugging.

"Just red? No, no, no. Just Red is a different color. That's **Firetruck Full of Apples.**" Grandpa Pepper reached for the orange marker Herbert was using that on any other day would've been called . . . orange. "And this is **Cheddar Cheese in Florida.**"

"In **Florida?**" Portico cocked his head.

"Yeah, where oranges grow," Grandpa Pepper confirmed.

Portico looked at Zola for a little help. He'd only known Grandpa Pepper for a few minutes and could already tell he was the strangest old man he'd ever met. Even stranger than Mr. Mister, and Mr. Mister was pretty strange.

"I thought this was red. It is, right?" Portico asked, shyly.

Zola laughed. "Grandpa Pepper, can you cut it out?"

"I'm sorry, Zola. You know I can't stop working." **Working?**

"Grandpa Pepper is the guy who comes up with names for nail polishes. He always thinking about colors, but, in a different way."

"Wait . . . that's somebody's **job**?" Herbert asked.

Grandpa Pepper held out his fingers and gave them a wiggle, his painted nails a party on his hands.

"**My** job. And the **best** job, Air Bear. **The BEST!**"

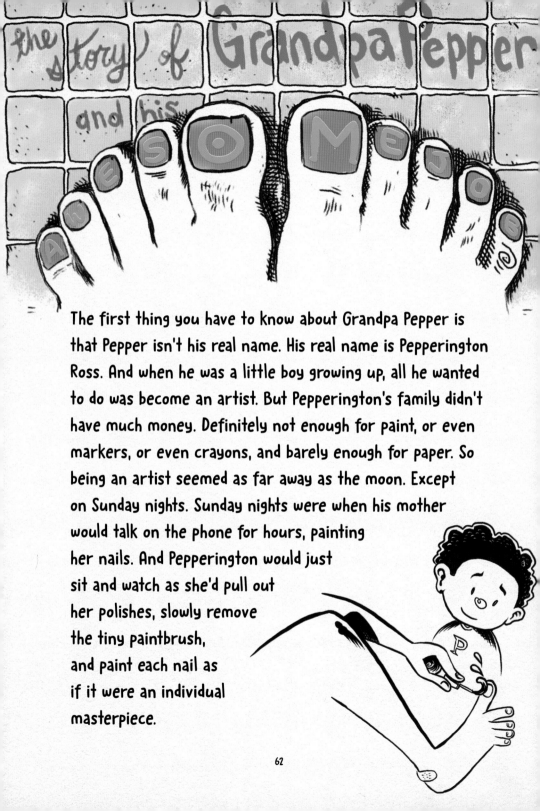

The story of Grandpa Pepper and his AWESOME JOE

The first thing you have to know about Grandpa Pepper is that Pepper isn't his real name. His real name is Pepperington Ross. And when he was a little boy growing up, all he wanted to do was become an artist. But Pepperington's family didn't have much money. Definitely not enough for paint, or even markers, or even crayons, and barely enough for paper. So being an artist seemed as far away as the moon. Except on Sunday nights. Sunday nights were when his mother would talk on the phone for hours, painting her nails. And Pepperington would just sit and watch as she'd pull out her polishes, slowly remove the tiny paintbrush, and paint each nail as if it were an individual masterpiece.

One day, he asked her if he could paint one of his own.

"Of course you can, Pepper. What color you want to try?"

"Red," he replied, pointing to the red polish.

"Red?" His mother scoffed. "That's not red. That's actually Stop Sign in the Middle of a Rose Garden on Valentine's Day." She said it as if he was supposed to know it already. As if everyone knew the difference between red and . . . all that. Also, she hadn't made that up trying to be funny.

"See? Says it right there, printed on the label: Stop Sign in the Middle of a Rose Garden on Valentine's Day."

That just made Pepperington want to try the color more. So he tried painting one of his nails. Turns out, he was a terrible artist. I mean, TERRIBLE. But he never forgot the name of the polish, the polish he'd called . . . red. And decided forever and ever to always give colors (and everything and everyone) names that matched their magic.

HERE ARE SOME OTHER NAIL POLISH NAMES FOR BASIC COLORS, ACCORDING TO GRANDPA PEPPER

1. GREEN = FAKE GRASS IN THE SUBURBS

2. PURPLE = ALIEN SNOT

3. BLUE = Vintage Computer Screen

4. YELLOW = Old Sneaker Bottom

Portico, Zola, and Herbert continued to watch TV and draw *Super Space Warriors*. The whole time, Herbert tried to tell them what he'd been trying to tell them: about the secret thing he'd found on the eighth floor, but Grandpa Pepper kept laughing or screaming or gasping at the show. He was soooo into it.

Eventually, Grandpa Pepper tore himself away from the television and announced he was leaving the apartment, leaving them alone. "I'll be back in about an hour," he said.

"Where you going, Grandpa?" Zola asked.

"To see an old friend. And when you're my age, old friends are old . . . friends. And if you don't see 'em when you can, they might be cold friends." Grandpa Pepper chuckled, grabbed a bag of his nail polishes, and headed for the door.

FULL OF EVERYTHING (AND EVERYONE)

AT LAST Herbert could finally get his secret out. It practically burst out of him.

"Y'all ready for this?" Herbert wound up, giddy giddy. Portico and Zola nodded in anticipation. "Yesterday, I found . . .

an **empty** apartment up on the eighth floor. And it's **open**. Not, like, wide open, but unlocked. Which is basically open."

An empty apartment in Skylight Gardens was a gold mine! It was like a playground with no playground stuff. No swings, no monkey bars, no sliding boards. Just a big open space to run around. A sandbox with no sand. An arena for tag. There were **hardly ever** any empty apartments in the building, and if there were, no one ever had access to them except for Herbert's mother, Mrs. Heather. She had a key to every apartment in the castle because she worked in the rental office and was responsible for making sure each apartment had people living in it. And—until now, apparently—people did live in them.

"And you been in there?" Portico asked.

"Yep!" Herbert said. "My mother went to check it out after the Carters moved out."

"The Carters moved out?!" Portico and Zola said at the same time. Roman Carter was one of their friends. Not a best best. But a good. That's the way things go when you live in a castle. One day you wake up and **poof!** People are just . . . gone. Just packed up and moved out. And a day or two later someone new moves in.

Poof

"Yep. They gone," Herbert confirmed. "Roman probably ate his parents outta house and home."

"What's that mean?" Portico asked.

"I don't know but my mother always says I'm doing it," Herbert said. "Point is, we should go up there. It's amazing. Totally full of . . . nothing!"

"No way." Portico couldn't believe what he was hearing. "Nothing?" He could count the number of times he'd seen an empty apartment.

Once when his parents had cleaned out the old apartment.

Once when he and his mother had moved into their new apartment.

Once when he and his father had moved into **their** new apartment.

So, three times.

Zola turned to Portico. "Oh, dang. You gotta go to your dad's, right?"

"Uh . . . yeah, but I think he's sleeping. So, I can at least just check it out," Portico said. Then added, "I can bring my trash, right?"

"If you want," Herbert said, confused by the trash bag but focused on the goodie bag—the empty apartment.

On their way down the hall, Portico asked Herbert the most important question any friend could ask. A question Zola had asked Portico when they became friends. This question had been on Portico's mind since breakfast, and if it hadn't been for everything going on with his mother and father, he probably would've been thinking about it for as long as he and Herbert had been friends. So . . . for thirteen days.

"Herbert, I been meaning to ask you—if you could be a superhero, who would you be?" Portico asked.

"Huh?"

"If you could be a superhero, what superhero would you be?" Zola repeated.

"I'll be a Super Space Warrior too. There's two of 'em."

"I'm both."

"How can you be both?" Herbert asked.

"Because I can be as many people as I want," Zola replied. "So, now answer the question. Matter fact, a better question is, what's your super**power**?"

Herbert was stumped. "Umm . . . I don't know." He loved superheroes, but he could never see himself as one. A little guy. Kinda odd looking. Couldn't imagine himself as super or a hero. "What's yours, Portico?"

But Portico was too busy freaking out to answer. Because they were approaching the elevator. He wasn't in full fret mode, but he could feel his stomach tightening like a dishrag getting water wrung out. Luckily, Portico didn't get all the way to **scared** scared, because there was a big sign taped to the elevator doors:

OUT OF ORDER

Phew, thought Portico.

SCARY STAIR-Y

What Portico **hadn't** thought about was how—because the elevator was broken—everyone would have to take the steps. **EVERYONE.** Going up. Or going down. The kids, the elders, the weenagers, the treenagers, and the freenagers, all traffic jamming in between floors. Portico and Zola and Herbert scooted past them all. Lots of **'scuse me's** and **watch outs.** They got to the landing of the sixth floor. And there, they were met by the worst.

THE WORSTS

Look who it is! Herbert Singletary the SELLOUT!

a big boy named Butter, dressed in a one-piece pajama, said. He looked like he wasn't supposed to have on what he had on, but also

like he was totally supposed to have it on. With him were all the other ugly-stinkies.

J.J.J. whose face always looked like Portico's stomach felt— upset.

Stank Frank, whose name said it all.

Walnut Head, whose nickname used to be Peanut Head until his head kept growing.

Piano, whose mouth looked like piano keys, but ain't make a single good sound.

Slowdown, a motor mouth. Fastest talker in Skylight Gardens.

Car Seat Carrie, small, but always down for the ride.

And, Brian. Just . . . Brian.

the
WORSTS
aka
ugly-
Stinkies

TM and © copyright the Worsts and ugly-Stinkies! all rights reserved living or dead

"Wassup, Butter," Herbert said.

But instead of Butter responding, J.J.J. snapped back. "I see you hangin' out with your new friends, Shortico and . . . and . . . Glasses Girl."

"Wow, good one, J.J.J.," Portico scoffed. Glasses Girl? That was the best she could come up with? These were Herbert's old friends back when he was still Herbert Singletary the Worst. Back when he was still Portico's meanest weenaged bully, even though, technically, Herbert was the same age as Portico and Zola. He was just hanging out with older kids. And sure, it always seemed like he was the boss, but really Herbert was more like their chihuahua—a tiny terror, doing all the barking and all the biting. Which is why his old bullying buddies had clearly needed him to dish out their jokes. Now Herbert-less, their snaps just weren't snapping.

"We just want to get by. Just minding our business," Zola said.

"Where y'all going?" Butter asked.

"To wherever people go to mind their business," Zola fired back.

"Oh yeah?" J.J.J. folded her arms.

"Come on, y'all," Herbert said. "Just let us by."

"Or what?" Butter said threateningly.

While all this was going on, curiosity was scratching at Portico. "Wait . . . your mother named you . . . Butter?" Butter's face became Tomato Sauce Fruit Punch, which ain't nothing like the color of butter.

"No . . . I . . ."

The truth was, Portico wasn't trying to be funny—he loved

butter, especially on movie popcorn. But before he could say this, Butter gave the trash bag a kick like it was a soccer ball at recess.

The bag flew down the steps. Portico and Zola went chasing after it, yelling "Sorry!
Sorry!
Sorry!"
as it bopped a few people in the head, including Mr. Chico.

Butter turned his attention to Herbert, picking on him. As a matter of fact, he started picking **UP** him.

HERBERT SINGLETARY the CHUMP.

And on and on they went. Zola and Portico, bag in arms, were up in arms. Zola wanted to do something to help Herbert, but she didn't know what to do. Neither did Portico. The frets were kicking in big time. Portico's insides felt like he needed to hang a sign from them, like the sign taped to the elevator doors:

OUT of ORDER!

"We gotta do **something!**" Portico panicked.

"You know what this reminds me of?" Zola . . . un-panicked.

"Zola, later! We have to do **something!**" Portico repeated.

"Y'all! Do something!" Herbert yelled.

"But what? What would Mater and Pater do?" Zola asked.

"I don't know. But if Butter lets go of Herbert . . .
it's gonna be an . . .

Zola gave him a look. "He not gonna explode, Portico."

"Look how red he is. He might!"

"No . . . he won't, because that's not how humans work."

Zola might've been right about humans not exploding, but
Portico didn't hear it.

He'd already become Stuntboy, dipping and dodging all the people in the in-between like an obstacle course. He only had one stunt up his sleeve. Or up his pant leg.

Who knows where he keeps his stunts?! He tried to never do this stunt because it was tricky and was also pretty bad on the knees. Not as bad as the Hippo Hippity Hop Over, but close. The stunt was called the Clip Up Trip Up, and could only be done in a stairwell when running up the steps. So . . . **now!**

Up Portico went. Step by step. Step. Step. Step. And exactly when he got to the last one, Portico pulled the stunt. "Clip Up Trip Up!" he shouted, his voice echoing off the stairwell walls. Portico cut the final step short, stubbing his foot, lurching him forward. He flung the trash bag over his head. It slammed right into Butter's face. Butter let go of Herbert, making him Herbert Singletary the Saved. Zola grabbed Herbert, Portico grabbed the trash, and they kept on keeping on, running until they'd made it up up up to the eighth floor.

EPISODE 3

ART BROKEN

Roll credits.

Wait. Stop the credits! Stop the credits!

Who in the world is Jason Reynolds?
That's who we're giving the credit to? Jason Reynolds?

JASON REYNOLDS

Raúl the Third

And Raúl the Third? Are you serious? Who's that? Why not the Second? Where's Raúl the First? We don't do Thirds here!

Anyway, cue the theme music, but let's fix these credits please.

Wherever it says Jason Reynolds or Raúl the Third, let's put my name.

FULL OF NOTHING

"He only could do that because he's bigger than me," Herbert complained as they headed for the secret apartment. "If I were just seven inches taller, no way would he have even been able to do that, and then you wouldn't have had to—"

"Save you?" Portico blurted, feeling heroic.

"You ain't save me!" Herbert barked. "You helped me."

"Ah," Zola said. "So your superpower might be . . . lying?"

But Herbert Singletary the ~~Saved~~ Helped pretended he didn't hear her, and instead stopped in front of 8A, Roman Carter's old apartment. He looked to the left and to the right to make sure no one was coming. Then he knocked gently.

"I thought you said there was no one here," Portico said.

"There's not. But you gotta knock anyway. Give the rats a chance to run."

"Rats?!" Portico shouted. "There's rats in there?!"

"Shhhh! Who's scared now?" Herbert taunted. "Anyway, I'm

just joking." He turned the doorknob. He was right. The door was unlocked and opened with ease.

And there it was. An empty apartment, also known as the greatest place on Earth, or at least the greatest place in Skylight Gardens. Better than the view from a tenth floor window. Better than the courtyard. Better than the snack truck always parked out front where Portico picked up his salt and vinegar potato chips.

"Oh . . . my . . ." Zola immediately did a handstand and began walking on her hands around the empty space, nothing there to knock her over. Except Portico, who went around opening every door in the place. The bathroom doors. The bedroom doors. The cabinets. The closets. Every single one—even the refrigerator door—just so he could see what a completely empty place looked like. What it felt like.

Herbert was busy pulling markers and crayons from his pocket.

"You stole those from my house?" Zola asked, indignantly.

"Of course not," Herbert said. "I **borrowed** them. For this."

And before Zola could even get mad, Herbert Singletary the ~~Saved~~ ~~Helped~~ ~~Liar~~ Thief became Herbert Singletary the Artist and started drawing on . . . THE WALL!

COMMERCIAL: This commercial is brought to you by
THINGS TO NEVER DO IN AN EMPTY APARTMENT

1. Don't go in. I repeat, DON'T GO IN! Even if the door is unlocked. I think it's against the law. Okay . . . it's definitely against the law.

2. Don't draw all over the walls.

Now back to your regularly scheduled program.

DO NOT ENTER

But they were already in.

And . . . Herbert had already started drawing. ALL over the wall. And once Zola saw what was happening, she wanted in on the fun. So she grabbed a marker and started drawing on a different wall. Portico wasn't about to be left out, so he grabbed a marker and took a blank wall for himself. All three on three different walls, drawing their hearts out.

HMMM...

Or at least trying to. Portico was having a hard time coming up with anything.

He had a yellow marker, and every time he'd make a mark, he'd stop. Stuck. Then he'd start again. Stuck again. The only thing he was sure about was that he loved the color yellow. The color made him think of something.

"Herbert?" Portico called over his shoulder.

"Yeah?"

"Did Butter's mother really name him Butter?"

Herbert responded mid-masterpiece.

"Nah. She named him Butterfly."

"Butterfly?!" Zola shrieked.

"Butterfly. Even better," Portico said. Just like that, he was unstuck and began to scribble frantically. First, wings. Big wings. And then he drew them separating from the middle, four wings going separate ways and becoming separate two-winged butterflies, flying in circles. And the caterpillar was left, with long antennae, wandering around in circles too, as the butterflies that used to be connected to him became their own thing and did their own thing without him, or each other. He stepped back to look at it, frowned.

PORTICO'S drawing

Then Portico shook off the frown.

Then he drew a sloth. And he gave the sloth a unicorn horn.

Then he drew an ant. And put the caterpillar and ant in the sloth's paws.

"What is all that?" Herbert asked, looking up from his own art. He'd just finished drawing a house. Somewhere that wasn't Skylight Gardens. Someplace with . . . a portico.

"Well, these two-winged butterflies are my mom and dad. This caterpillar is me. And all this"—Portico pointed to the sloth and ant—"is y'all."

ZOLA BRAND
satisfaction
guaranteed
or your money
back!

Zola, who'd been drawing the most elaborate giant lawn chair ever, turned to see.

"Us?" she asked.

"Yep. That's me." Portico pointed at the caterpillar again. "And that's you, Herbert," he said, pointing to the ant.

"An ant?" Herbert seemed a little upset. A little . . . antsy. (Sorry, I couldn't help it!)

"Not just an ant. A **fire** ant. You think we should call you Fire Ant Boy?" But before Herbert could even think about that, Zola put her hand up.

"Wait." She came closer to get a better look. "Where am I?"

Portico pointed to the sloth. "Right here."

"What . . . is it?"

"What you mean? It's a sloth!" Portico couldn't understand how Zola couldn't tell a sloth was a sloth. It looked **just** like a sloth. At least to him it did.

"You think I'm a **sloth?**" Ohhh. Zola was offended. But to Portico this is what 216 days of friendship looked like.

"Yeah. You know, because you so chill."

"And hairy!" Herbert joked. Zola slapped him on the arm. Herbert ouched, then added, "Hey, what's growing out her head?"

"It's a unicorn horn," Portico explained. "Like, **obviously**. Because Zola the only Zola in the world. She basically a slothicorn."

"A slothicorn?" Zola wasn't sure how to feel about all this. But Portico just smiled and nodded, proud proud proud.

It wasn't just his art that made him happy, it was the whole experience. He and his friends in a place that

belonged to no one but them. Portico loved being with Zola and Herbert, in their own special apartment, feeling like they were a team. That's how it used to be with his parents for so long. Until things changed, and it was, SO LONG. He reached into his back pocket, wiggled out the magnet his grandmother had brought him—
WHAT HAPPENS IN VEGAS STAYS IN VEGAS—
and stuck it on the fridge.

This was **their** place now.

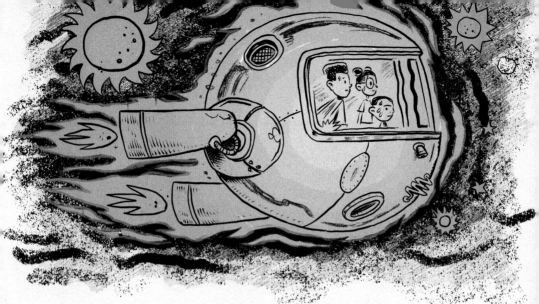

INSIDE THE SINGLETARY SUNJET

Have you ever wondered what it's like to be inside a spaceship? Yeah, me too. And Portico, too. And Zola, too. But not Herbert. Because he lived in one. No, not his half-door hideout on the fourth floor, but his real apartment on the eighth. Apartment 8H. Right down the hall from the empty one.

They all ended up there after apartment 8A—Roman Carter's old place—had gotten so hot they couldn't stand it anymore. They had no idea that when an apartment is empty, there's no reason to have an air conditioner on. So after about an hour of what had to be the funnest art project of all time—slothicorns!—Portico and his friends could barely move because their clothes were so sticky with sweat. Also, they were so desperate for a cold drink that before they left, Portico ran over to the sink in the empty apartment and drank right from the faucet. Zola refused to drink from the sink. Herbert too, but for different reasons. For Zola, she felt that if water didn't come from a spring, it must be dirty. Sure, the castle water was a little cloudy at first, but if you waited ten seconds, it'd become crystal clear. Portico's father always said the cloudiness was just minerals and that minerals were good for you. Like vitamins. Yum.

Herbert, on the other hand, wanted nothing to do with the water coming out of the tap, not because it was dirty (it wasn't dirty!) but because it was . . . water.

"Water don't taste like nothing," he grumped as they slipped out of the the empty apartment and headed down to his. "It's like drinking air. It's just wet invisibleness. Even burps taste better than water."

"You clearly have never had spring water, especially out of a bottle," Zola said.

"That don't even make sense," Herbert said. "You think water, **any** kind of water, tastes better than juice?"

"What kind of juice?" Portico asked.

"Any kind of juice!"

JUICES BETTER THAN WATER (ACCORDING TO HERBERT SINGLETARY THE JUICE DRINKER):

1. Pickle juice

2. Tomato juice

3. Beetlejuice (Beetlejuice, Beetlejuice!)

good
Ol' Dill
brand pickle juice

SHAMBLES

TOMATO
JUICE

BEETLE JUICE!
BEETLE JUICE!
BEETLE JUICE!

Herbert opened the door to his apartment. His mom's apartment. But to Portico and Zola, the most important person who lived there was Portico's stepfather, Soup. THEE super.

And Soup's apartment was exactly what you'd expect a super's apartment to look like.

THINGS A SUPER (SHORT FOR SUPERINTENDENT WHICH IS REALLY LONG FOR SUPER WHICH IS ACTUALLY SHORT FOR SUPERHERO BUT SECRET IDENTITIES ARE IMPORTANT) HAS IN THEIR APARTMENT ACCORDING TO PORTICO REEVES:

1. Furniture that was shaped funny. The coffee table, which was supposed to be a rectangle, was a circle instead. Maybe that's what tea tables are like. And the couch looked like a cockpit.

2. A kitchen faucet that could transform into a hose.

3. A dishwasher . . . there was a dishwasher!

4. A refrigerator that could make ice (in three ways), and also could make water!

"Wait, does your spaceship fridge make **food**, too?" Portico parked his trash bag down by the front door and joined Herbert and Zola in the kitchen. Herbert was leaning into the fridge, moving all kinds of food out the way to get to the juice. Portico had never seen so much food in a refrigerator. And not one pea in sight. Carrot either. **Whoa.**

Herbert poured himself a glass of juice. Peach juice, which Portico had never even heard of. He poured a glass for Zola, too. But before he could pour a glass for Portico, Portico refused. "Water for me, please."

"Gross," Herbert said.

"Not if you got an imagination." So Herbert poured Portico a glass of water from the fridge faucet. Took way longer to fill a glass with fridge water than it did getting water from the sink. Also . . . no minerals. Hmm.

"Let's make a toast," Zola suggested.

"Perfect. I'm starving," Portico said. "Herbert's refrigerator can probably make it for us."

"No, a toast. A cheers," Zola said, raising her glass. "To our new apartment."

"TO OUR NEW APARTMENT!"

They all sat in the living room, and with each sip of water, Portico imagined he was drinking something else.

"Okay, Portico! We get it," Zola said, laughing. And even though Portico was being silly (he really wasn't being silly, he was being serious, but his serious was silly, seriously) he couldn't laugh because he was too busy looking around Herbert's living room. Not at the furniture. He'd already seen all that. But at the pictures on the wall, and the ones propped up on the tea table in frames. Pictures of Herbert's mother and Soup, arms around each other. Pictures of them with Herbert on what must've been vacation because there was no sand in Skylight Gardens and Portico wasn't sure he'd ever seen sun that bright before. Pictures on rides at amusement parks, and on airplanes. And even though Herbert wasn't smiling in every picture, all Portico could think about were the photos

he had like this. Or the photos he used to have like this. The pictures of Herbert's smiling parents were making Portico think of how his own parents used to be. Of how his apartment used to look. The ones with him and his mother and father hugged up in the lobby of Skylight Gardens during one of his mother's famous Hair Cut Days. Or the photo of the three of them standing in front of the movie theater the first time Portico's mother and father had taken him. Or their first (and last) time at the zoo. In that one, Portico was angry because of all the animals being locked up, but . . . he was still cute. Or the one when they first got their pet cat,

A New Name Every Day. Or the one with Gran Gran on her last day as a nurse.

But now there were no pictures on the walls. Not anymore. His imagination was only seeing frowns, making his water taste just like them.

Lemon juice.

Then hot sauce.

Then vinegar.

IN CASE YOU WERE
WONDERING . . .

Your imagination can change the way
everything tastes. Food. Water. Life.

Which is why you should eat your peas and
carrots. Just imagine they're french fries.

SUPER DISTRACTED

"I have another toast," Herbert said. "To our eighth-floor
masterpiece!"

"Cheers!"

"Cheers!"

They clanked their glasses. Took another sip. That had been
the tenth toast. There was hardly anything left in their cups,
but they kept pretending there was, which was perfect for
Portico because he'd been doing that the whole time anyway.

"Your turn, Portico," Zola said.

"Um . . ." Portico thought for a moment. He'd already toasted to his superpower and his bag of trash, and he thought about toasting to his parents, but wasn't sure he could do that without turning into water himself. "Um . . ."

Just then, the front door of Herbert's apartment opened. In came Soup.

Portico grinned. "Toast to . . . the super!"

"Cheers!" Zola said, raising her glass.

"Cheers," Herbert said, less enthusiastic.

Soup was on the phone, but when Portico and his friends lifted their glasses, the super paused for a second and smiled as if he really needed that toast. Or maybe needed some toast. It was almost noon, which meant almost lunch time, and it didn't look like the super would have a chance to eat anytime soon.

"Honey, I'm **trying**," he said, stepping over Portico's bag. "I just can't fix it. The elevator repairman is supposed to get here soon. Huh? Herbie? He's right here with his friends. No . . . not **those** friends."

"Hi, Mom!" Herbert called out.

"Sweetheart, I gotta go. Bean Bosworth woke up this morning and realized her whole apartment is full of iguanas, and now she wants me to come get them out."

"Iguanas?" Portico whispered to Zola. And as soon as Soup got off the phone, Portico said it again, louder. **"Iguanas?"**

"Iguanas," the super confirmed. "Bean's been buying a new iguana every week for months. Collecting them or something. But this morning she woke up and freaked out because her place is . . . full of . . . iguanas.

She says she's scared one is gonna get stuck in the sink, or the toilet, or who knows where else."

Portico couldn't believe what he was hearing. Mainly because he **loved** iguanas! Okay, he'd never actually **seen** an iguana. He'd also never seen Bean Bosworth even though she lived at the end of his old floor. 4Q. The same floor Zola still lived on. The same floor Herbert's boiler room was on. How had none of them ever seen Bean Bosworth? Or an iguana?

THE BONKERS RUMOR ABOUT BEAN BOSWORTH

I don't know if this is true. No one does. Not even Portico. But the rumor about Bean Bosworth is that every time she leaves her apartment, she puts on a completely different disguise. That way, she always looks like a person visiting Bean Bosworth, and not like Bean Bosworth herself.

Not sure if this is true either, but people think the reason she does this is because it makes her seem like the most popular person on the fourth floor. But now, after hearing what the super was saying, I think maybe she does it so no one knows she's been buying so many iguanas.

Bonkers!

REPTILE RECRUITMENT

Soup ran to the kitchen, grabbed a glass, and filled it with water. From the faucet. He guzzled it down.

"Ahhhhhhhhhhhhhhhhh. . . ."

"Told y'all," Portico said.

After belching loud enough to **shake the walls,**

the super asked, "Y'all want to help me wrangle some lizards?"

"Nope!" Herbert said.

"Come on, Herbert," Zola said. **"Iguanas! We have to!"**

Herbert sighed. "Okay, fine."

"You in, Portico?" the super asked.

"He's headed down to his dad's place," Herbert said.

"Yeah, I mean, I am, but . . . he wouldn't want me to leave y'all to clean up all them iguanas, especially since cleaning up is kinda his job," Portico said, shutting Herbert down. "But is it okay if I bring my trash?"

COMMERCIAL BREAK: This commercial is brought to you by
THINGS TO (SECRETLY) NAME YOUR PET TRASH BAG

1. Trash Bag. Not a bad name.
2. Trashy.
3. Baggy.
4. Junky Junk.
5. Veggie.
6. Mr. Hackensack, which also happens to be the name of Portico's teacher.

Now back to your regularly scheduled program.

A FEW FOLKS IN THE WAY OF THE IGUANAS

Going to see, and hopefully free, an apartment full of iguanas was exciting, but what was just as exciting for Portico was being able to take the stairwell with no fear, because Soup was with them and nobody messed with Soup. **Nobody.**

The stairwell was as busy as it had been earlier. People inching up and down the steps, others just hanging out. Rena Simms had set up a lemonade stand with no lemonade. Just water and sugar. She said all you had to do was find your own lemons and boom! Lemonade!

Pinky Walsh was singing at the top of his lungs, in a language he'd made up.

Mr. Davis was covered in oil and **lugging a car engine strapped to his back** up the steps, which was weird because there was no way he was building a car in his apartment.

Okay . . . he might've totally been building a car in his apartment!

And this person and that person, all trying to get Soup's attention to tell him about the things they needed. But he told everyone the same thing:

"I'll get to it after I deal with these iguanas!"

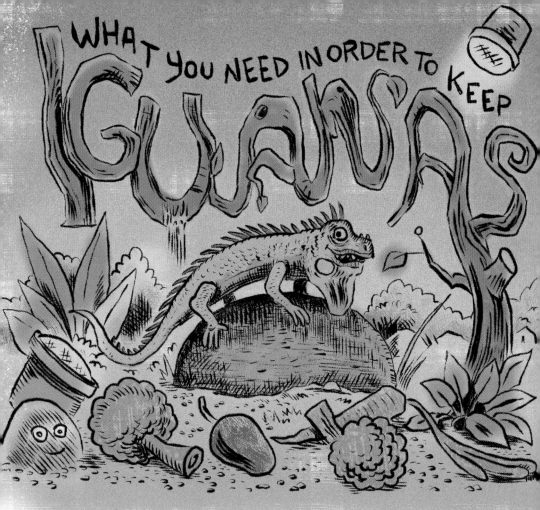

1. Some kind of case—aquarium, terrarium—for them to live in unless you want them on your kitchen table.
2. Lots of veggies. That's what they like to eat. Because they clearly have never had Portico's famous (since this morning) Unhealthy Oatmeal. Ain't no way they'd choose veggies over sugar.
3. A special light. The UV kind. UV stands for ultraviolet. It's like sun if the sun was inside. Bright and hot. And Iguanas need sun. Even if it's fake.

HOW BEAN BOSWORTH KEPT IGUANAS

1. She didn't. They kept her. In her bedroom.

The thing about Bean Bosworth was that because no one ever really saw her, no one knew how old she was. But judging by her furniture, Portico guessed she was at least Gran Gran's age. The couch had plastic on it, which only old people do. The carpet was burgundy, which Portico had never seen in an any apartment in Skylight Gardens. Not burgundy carpet . . . but carpet at all! Old people. And she had a special cabinet just for her white plates, which Portico had only seen in . . . you guessed it . . . old people's apartments. He was never sure why certain plates got special treatment, especially since they hadn't been drawn on, or painted on, or anything. The point is, if it was true that Bean Bosworth was old, that would explain why she'd be pretty freaked out by all those lizards.

They were everywhere. Some climbing onto the window sills, others onto the chairs. Some were even skittering across the coffee table. Gran Gran would've had a fit!

"What . . . the . . ." Herbert was frazzled but trying to play tough as usual.

SEVENTEEN PETS WORSE THAN SEVENTEEN IGUANAS

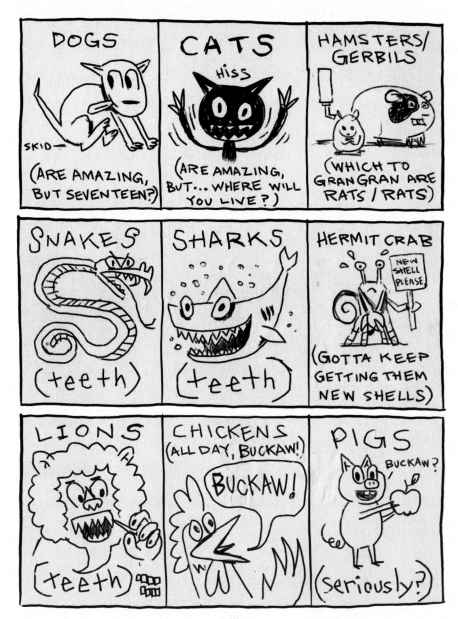

BULLS

(HORNS)

ROACHES

(gross)

RACCOONS

Like furry roaches
that act like humans.

SQUIRRELS

(too squirrelly)

MICE

(AGAIN, TO GRAN GRAN
...RATS)

ROCKS

(. . .)

HERBERTS

(Because one is more
than enough)

tRASH

BAGS

Collect them
all! Hide
them under
your bed or
in your under-
wear drawer!
Don't tell your
parents! Shhhh!

Soup prepared Portico, Zola, and Herbert for the task.

"I don't have any proper traps, so we're gonna have to use our hands. Let me show you all how to do it." And then Soup pounced on one of the iguanas that had been crawling right beside him. You would've thought he was wrestling an alligator, but the iguana couldn't have been much bigger than one of Portico's sneakers. "Make sure . . . you grab it . . . right under the chin, here," Soup said, out of breath and holding the iguana up, the tail whipping back and forth. Soup opened a trash bag, gently placed the first one in, then wiped sweat from his forehead. At this rate, Soup was bound to break a leg or hurt his back or something. Portico could tell that Soup, though super, clearly wasn't trained in iguana catching. Or stunting, like he was.

One down, **sixteen** to go.

Then, Soup's phone rang.

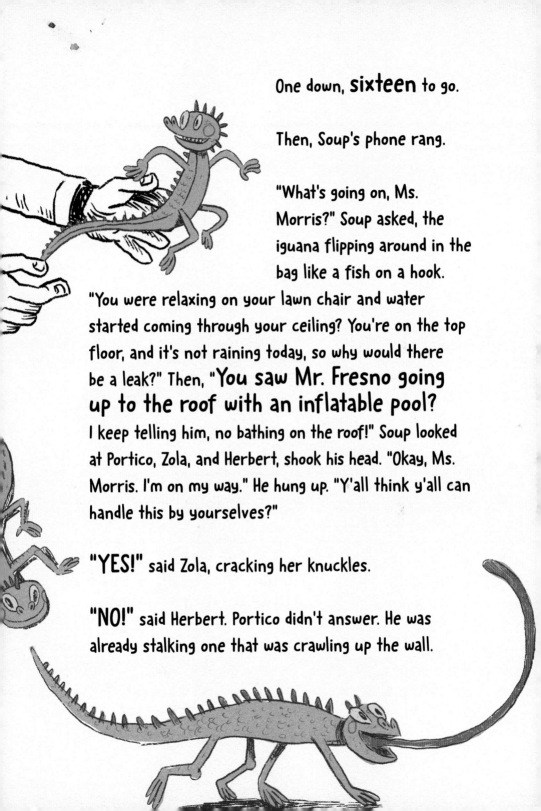

"What's going on, Ms. Morris?" Soup asked, the iguana flipping around in the bag like a fish on a hook. "You were relaxing on your lawn chair and water started coming through your ceiling? You're on the top floor, and it's not raining today, so why would there be a leak?" Then, "**You saw Mr. Fresno going up to the roof with an inflatable pool?** I keep telling him, no bathing on the roof!" Soup looked at Portico, Zola, and Herbert, shook his head. "Okay, Ms. Morris. I'm on my way." He hung up. "Y'all think y'all can handle this by yourselves?"

"**YES!**" said Zola, cracking her knuckles.

"**NO!**" said Herbert. Portico didn't answer. He was already stalking one that was crawling up the wall.

SIXTEEN
HOW TO CATCH ~~SEVENTEEN~~ IGUANAS

As soon as Soup left, Herbert stood in a corner and decided not to help. At all.

"I'm sorry, y'all. I just can't do it," he said. While Portico eyed the iguana on the wall, Zola took a good look at Herbert and realized he just didn't have it in him.

"It's cool," Zola said. "Me and Portico will get—"

Portico dove for the iguana, knocking a picture of Bean Bosworth off the wall. At least they assumed it was Bean Bosworth. The person in the picture had their hand in front of their face.

"Portico! What you **doing?**" Zola scolded.

"Sorry, sorry," Portico said. The iguana he'd been chasing scurried across the wall. Still free.

"Everything okay out there?" Bean called. "They not eating y'all, are they?"

"No, they not eating us," Zola said. She turned to Portico, spoke under her breath. "Let me handle this."

WHAT NO ONE KNEW
ABOUT ZOLA BRAWNER

Portico stood back while Zola got down and eased up to an iguana who was crawling around the carpet as if it were a patch of burgundy grass. She closed her eyes like she was about to start meditating, gave a long blink, then, ZWAP! grabbed the iguana in a half of a half of a half of a second. It happened so fast Portico thought he'd missed it.

"Bag," she called. Portico and Herbert held the bag open. Fifteen left.

"Yo, what kind of meditation is **that**?" Portico asked. Zola ignored him, eased toward the next one, which had crawled up the leg of the coffee table. The lizard looked to the left, to the right, totally unaware of what was coming.

ZWAP! Got 'im! Zola put that one gently in the bag with the other two.

The one climbing the wall that Portico'd missed, Zola needed to jump to get. ZWAP! And got.

One was under the couch. Zola got down on her belly and iguana-ed over to the . . . iguana.

ZWAP! Twelve to go.

ZWAP!
              ZWAP!
                         ZWAP! over and over and
over again, from the living room, into the kitchen, and even
in the bathroom, until the bag was completely full of Bean
Bosworth's lizard colony.

It took no time at all. Sixteen minutes, tops.

NOW WHAT?

After the iguanas were all caught (and counted) the next thing was to figure out where to take them.

"We could throw 'em down the trash chute," Herbert said.

"**No way!**" Portico tied a knot in the lizard bag. "I don't wanna scare my dad when he finds a moving bag down there."

"Hello!?! They're **animals**. Can't just throw them away," Zola added.

"Right. That too," Portico agreed. He thought for a moment. "How about we take them outside and release them?"

"And let them just run around the property?" Herbert was concerned.

Portico imagined the snack truck covered in iguanas. "Yeah, you right. Bad idea."

"I don't want to get **rid** of them," Bean Bosworth said, scaring Portico, Zola, and Herbert because they hadn't heard her come from her room—she just appeared—and on top of that they weren't expecting to see her with her face covered in a thick orange-ish clay that made her look just like . . . an iguana.

Portico had seen his mother wear those masks. Looked like she smeared cake batter all over her face, which meant, to him, it looked like fun.

"I mean, I thought I did, but now that they're all in that bag, I realize how . . . how . . . **empty** my apartment is without them." She burst into tears and took off back into her bedroom, leaving Portico holding the bag. **Oof.**

ROOM FOR SEVENTEEN

Where could the iguanas go?

Where, oh where?

They couldn't go in the fridge. Too cold.
They couldn't go in the trash can because trash has to go in there, and iguanas ain't trash.

They couldn't go in the closet. Too dark.

Maybe the bathtub? Nah, they ain't like rubber duckies.

Where could the iguanas go?

Portico looked around the room, pondering, pondering.
Until it hit him.

"I got an idea."

"Uh-oh," Herbert said.

"What you think—?" Zola said, but before she could even

get it all the way out, Portico was already standing in front of the cabinet with the white plates. "Portico, no."

"Yep," Portico said. "It's just like Episode 103 of *Super Space Warriors* when Mater and Pater first met Frater and Soror, and how Frater and Soror were part of a bunch of other trainees competing to be on the team. And Mater and Pater were only looking for one new member. One new warrior.

But both Frater and Soror were good."

"And they were brother and sister," Zola said.

"And then there was . . .

AN EXPLOSION OF GREAT MAGNITUDE!" Herbert shouted.

"No . . . Herbert. There wasn't," Portico replied. "Mater and Pater let them both join. Made enough space for both of them in the Sun Fortress. Because . . . um . . . because families belong together."

"Oh . . . right," Herbert said. Portico turned back to the dish cabinet.

The upside was that Portico thought the white plates in the cabinet were fancy until he opened the glass door to remove them, afraid the iguanas would shatter them all. But then he realized they were . . . Styrofoam! He pulled them all out anyway, but for a different reason.

"Herbert, you still got the markers?"

HOME DECOR

What they drew on the plates:

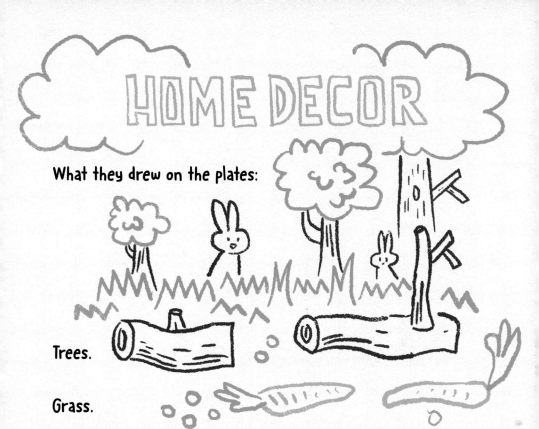

Trees.

Grass.

Big logs.

Carrots and peas.

The Statue of Liberty. Not sure why, but Portico drew it.

And other iguanas. Family photos.

Once the decorations were all done, every iguana was placed in the glass case. **The lizard castle.** Then Portico aimed the UV lamps to shine into the case. Fake sun.

Episode 4
HOW TO MAKE A FISH BONE A WISHBONE

Okay everybody, let's break for lunch!

(Oh, shoot. Cue the music or they won't turn the page!)

Welcome to Stuntboy In-Between Time

IGUANA'D UP AN APPETITE

Once they finished saving the iguanas, Portico, Zola, and Herbert were met by an **amazing** smell coming from Zola's apartment door. They were all hungry, and that smell hooked its fingers into their noses and pulled them inside.

Music was playing. The kind of music Gran Gran loved. Old-school stuff with horns in it. And the people growling more than they sing. Basically, the music sounded like a funky orchestra of bears and ducks.

There were shoes at the door. A pair of old dress shoes and a pair of slippers suspiciously like the ones Gran Gran called her "outside slippers."

And there was laughter coming from the kitchen. High, shrieky laughter that sounded just like the laughter of . . . Gran Gran?

"Grandpa Pepper, I'm back!" Zola called out, kicking her sneakers off. Grandpa Pepper stepped out of the kitchen, an apron tied around his waist, a goofy, poofy hat on his head.

"Good afternoon, Madame Zola!" he said in a terrible accent. "Ah. And to you two as well, Monsieur Porchie and Monsieur Air Bear."

"Smells good in here, Mr. Grandpa Pepper," Portico said, releasing the plastic tail of his trash bag.

"It should!" a voice called from the kitchen. Not just any voice, but a grandmother's voice. And not just any grandmother's voice, but a **Gran Gran's** voice. "I'm doing magical things."

"Gran Gran, what you doing here?" Portico asked, surprised to see her.

"What **you** doing here?" Gran Gran replied. "Your dad just called me looking for you. Don't worry, I covered for you **this** time and told him you were probably running around with your friends. But you better get down there." The thing about Gran Gran is she's always good about making sure to look the other way whenever Portico is doing something he isn't supposed to be doing. But she would only do it once. She said if she covered for him more than once in a single day, then she'd basically become one of his little friends. And even though she was his friend, she was not one of his **little** friends. There was a difference, and Portico knew exactly what she meant.

"I will, I will. But first, I had to save—"

"**Ahem.**" Zola pretended to clear her throat.

"Sorry, I had to help **Zola** save seventeen iguanas."

"Been there, done that," Grandpa Pepper said.

Portico looked at Zola. She shrugged.

"Grandpa Pepper, how you know Ms. Gran Gran?" Zola asked.

"I told you I had to go check on an old friend," Grandpa Pepper said, pointing at Portico's grandmother.

"Who you calling old?" Gran Gran jabbed. Then she came over and gave Portico a tight hug. "What, you thought you were the only person with friends? I've known Pepper longer than I've known you!" she said, still squeezing him. She pulled away for a second to show Portico her freshly painted nails—Cotton Candy on a Rainy Day—then kissed him on his forehead. And one kiss leads to another and another, especially for grandmas, so she went down the line, forehead-smooching.

"And you," she said to Zola. **"Muah."**

"And . . . even though I don't know you like that yet," she said to Herbert. **"Muah."**

"That's Herbert Singletary. The Super's son," Portico said.

"Stepson," Herbert shot back.

"Ahhhh, you Soup's kid. Got any word on when that elevator's gonna be fixed?" Gran Gran asked.

"Yeah, because it took us at least thirty minutes to get this food up all them steps," Grandpa Pepper added.

"Took **you** thirty minutes. Because you old, Pepper. **You** old!" Gran Gran razzed, then turned back to the kids. "Y'all hungry?"

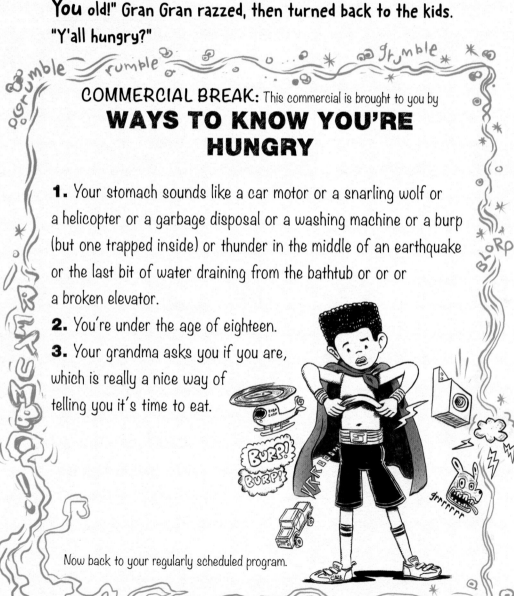

COMMERCIAL BREAK: This commercial is brought to you by

WAYS TO KNOW YOU'RE HUNGRY

1. Your stomach sounds like a car motor or a snarling wolf or a helicopter or a garbage disposal or a washing machine or a burp (but one trapped inside) or thunder in the middle of an earthquake or the last bit of water draining from the bathtub or or or a broken elevator.

2. You're under the age of eighteen.

3. Your grandma asks you if you are, which is really a nice way of telling you it's time to eat.

Now back to your regularly scheduled program.

WHAT'S ON THE MENU?

Normally, for Portico, lunch was lunch. You know, a baloney sandwich and a bag of chips. But the way that sandwich and chips played out all depended on who was preparing the lunch.

If Portico was making it himself, he would just put baloney between two pieces of bread. But not just one slice of baloney. More like ten slices.

Whenever his mother made the sandwich, she always put a single slice of baloney, and always always always added extra lettuce and tomato, which Portico always always always took off. She also gave the sandwich a haircut—removed the crust.

Whenever Portico's father made the sandwich, he always used two slices of baloney, with a piece of cheese between them, and he smeared mayo, ketchup, and mustard on the bread.

Whenever Gran Gran made the sandwich, she would fry the baloney, toast the bread, and put a little syrup on it.

The chips never changed.

Salt and vinegar.

Whole bag.

That was lunch. Usually. But not today. Today, Gran Gran and Grandpa Pepper were cooking up a feast in Zola's kitchen. Fried fish, macaroni and cheese, cornbread—which, to Portico, was way better than any version of a baloney sandwich. Only thing that was weird was that when Gran Gran started putting the food on the plates, the colors were all wrong.

Fried fish, macaroni and cheese, and cornbread were all supposed to be orange. Portico had had this kind of food before on special occasions—holidays, Gran Gran's birthday, family reunions. And it had **always** been orange. Usually even came with a cup of orange soda. But.

The fish was blue.

The macaroni was green.

The cornbread was purple.

"What's this?" Portico asked, poking at the fish.

"It's fish. You been eating fish your whole life."

"But it ain't never been **blue**." Portico sniffed it.

"You mean Blueberry Ocean," Grandpa Pepper said. Then he pointed to the macaroni and the cornbread. "And Wet Dollar, and Fig Skin."

Herbert didn't care what color the food was. He was chomping and scarfing. So was Zola. And after Portico saw

his friends stuffing their faces, he did the same. And it all tasted as good as the orange versions.

Then he took a sip of the orange soda and almost passed out.

"What's wrong with this orange soda?" Portico gasped. "I mean . . . besides y'all made it **clear!**"

"That's not orange soda!" Gran Gran said. "That's sparkling water."

Portico looked into his cup. "But it ain't sparkling. Or is that the name of the clear color?"

Gran Gran laughed. "No. That's just what they call it. It's like fizzy. I like to think of it as water . . . that **dances**." Gran Gran threw her hands in the air and busted a move to the old-school music with all the horns in it.

So did Grandpa Pepper.

But neither of them ate.

Apparently there were only three fish, and Portico and his friends were served one each. Portico offered his grandmother some of his fish, but she refused.

"Don't worry about us. We've got two more coming. Mrs. Fiona's son is running down to the fish market right now."

FIONA'S FISH

Mrs. Fiona lived on the third floor, and sold fish out of her apartment. Well, she was a sailor and fisherwoman, owned a fish market, but always kept a freezer full of fish handy so the older people in the building could just come buy it from 3R instead of walking the three blocks to the fish market. And everyone knew that if your cat ever got out of your apartment, there was a good chance you'd find it standing outside her door, begging. A New Name Every Day has been caught down there, playing extra cute, hoping a few fish guts would fall from Mrs. Fiona's apron.

Portico picked at his fish, making sure not to swallow the bones. He'd swallowed one once and it caused the frettiest frets ever. Something he **never** wanted to experience again. So he always took his time when eating fish. Herbert was chomping and scarfing like he'd never had a fret in the world, and guess what?

He got a bone stuck in his throat!

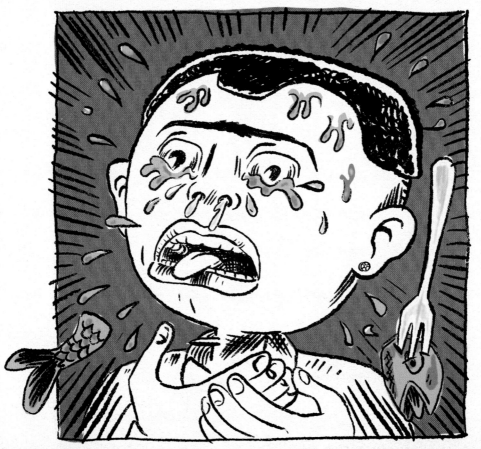

WHAT IT FEELS LIKE TO HAVE A FISH BONE IN YOUR THROAT

1. Like your spit is made of nails. The kind you hammer. Also maybe the kind that grows on fingers.

2. Like tiny lightning that strikes the same place way more than twice.

3. Like swallowing a fish bone.

WHAT TO DO WHEN YOU HAVE A FISH BONE IN YOUR THROAT

1. If you're Gran Gran, you swallow big chunks of bread to push it down. She even puts peanut butter on the bread to make it extra thick. Portico had seen her do it one time and it's also how he got the fish bone stuck in his throat unstuck. But Portico hadn't been choking so, in this case:

2. If you're Herbert Singletary the Choking . . . you are not okay. And you cry.

As Herbert burst into tears in fear that he'd spend the rest of his life with a fish bone stuck in his throat, there was a knock at the door. Gran Gran had gone to get some bread while Zola was trying to calm Herbert down.

"You are, Herbert. You have to envision it. My mother calls it manifesting."

"Okay, okay," Herbert panted. "What kind of fish am I?"

Zola looked at Portico. Portico at Zola. Neither of them knew what fish to say because they couldn't think of any kind of fish. Every time Portico ate it, his grandmother just called it fried fish.

There was another knock on the door, but they were too focused on Herbert to answer it.

"Um . . . Portico, what kind of fish is he?" Zola asked, looking for a little help.

"Bread's coming!" Grandpa Pepper called from the kitchen.

Another knock.

Portico took a sip of his dancing water and thought, *What fish could he be? What fish? What fish?*

"How about . . . a whale!" he said.

"A whale?" Herbert choked out.

"A whale?" Zola asked.

"A whale?" Gran Gran called from the kitchen.

"Yeah, because he could blow it right out his—"

"His **what**?" Zola cut him off.

"His . . . um . . . nose?"

"My nose?!" Herbert squawked.

Another knock.

"Can someone please get the door!" Grandpa Pepper shouted.

THE WORST SURPRISE

Portico could smell it before he opened the door. But he opened it anyway. And there he was: Stank Frank. Son of Mrs. Fiona. In his hands were two fish wrapped in paper. And he smelled like he'd just climbed out of his mother's freezer.

"You?" he said, taking a step forward, but Portico bravely blocked the door.

"Who is it?" Grandpa Pepper sang.

"It's . . . your fish," Portico said.

"Yo, is that . . . Herbert?" Stank Frank craned his neck to see around Portico, but Portico mimicked his every move, a stunt called the Misfit Mirror he'd perfected just a few days ago. He didn't want Stank Frank to see Herbert sobbing while Gran Gran fed him chunks of bread. Not a good look. So when Frank moved left, Portico moved left. Well, Portico moved right, which was Frank's left. He matched him. When Frank moved right, Portico matched him. When Frank got slick, and moved left-right, Portico did the same.

Up. Up.　　　　Up-　　　　UP-

Down. Down.　　　Down.　　　DOWN.

Down-up-left-diagonal-tippy toe. Down-up-left-diagonal-tippy toe. Portico stayed with him until all of a sudden, an unexpected, terrifying sound came up from the air vent:

AN EXPLOSION OF GREAT MAGNITUDE!

But this one had nothing to do with *Super Space Warriors*. Instead it was Mrs. Fiona, Stank Frank's mom, who also happened to have the loudest voice in Skylight Gardens.

She was right. It didn't take all day to deliver two fish. But Stank Frank was trying to deliver two fish and, oh, I don't know, at least a dozen mean jokes. And that takes time.

The rumor is, Mrs. Fiona's big voice comes from spending so much time on fishing boats and having to scream over the motor. Portico always figured she was so good at catching fish because all she had to do was yell at them and they'd jump right out of the water. And that's exactly what Stank Frank looked like: a fish out of water, flopping around at the sound of his mother's voice. So startled that he'd dropped the fish right where he was standing—they were not flopping around—and took off. Portico picked them up, still safely wrapped in paper.

"Thanks for stopping by," Portico mocked as Franklin hurried down the hall.

(Also . . . Branzino? Really?)

Episode 5   WALK LIKE A WEIRDO

Roll credits. Cue theme music.

Hey, we can keep the music the same, but can we change up
the graphics on the screen? Let's do something cool.
How about graffiti style?

Right?

Love it!

And a one, and a two, and . . .

WeLLLlllLcoMe to

IN-BETWEEN TIME!

GO . . . FISH?

The funny thing about getting fish bones stuck in your throat is that they're basically just like the frets. They're **pokey**, and really uncomfortable for a while, but usually they just . . . go down. Now, I don't know what happens when they get down into your belly. I mean, it ain't like it's normal to just be swallowing bones. And when you do, that means your body—which is already **full** of bones (206 to be exact!)—all of a sudden has an **extra** bone in it. And not a human bone, but a fish bone! Which maybe means you've become **part fish**. And if **that's** true, then Herbert Singletary the Crying (and Choking) became Herbert Singletary the Boy-Fish, which would make . . . for a perfect superhero name!

"Boy-Fish? Are you serious?" Herbert gasped. Portico and Zola had just finished their lunch—Herbert was grateful the bread had worked but he wouldn't touch any more fish—and now they were all in the kitchen washing dishes. Portico on scrub. Herbert on rinse. Zola on drying.

"Yeah, man! I mean, you swallowed the bone, and now it just lives in you, and maybe it's gonna give you a superpower," Portico said. He was pretty pleased he'd come up with the idea and was hoping Herbert would like it. Zola was already in. She loved it!

"Like breathing underwater!" Zola said with a bunch of duh in her voice.

"Why would I need to do that?"

"Why **wouldn't** you need to do that?" Portico flicked Herbert with water, which, of course, started a water fight, which, of course, ended with Gran Gran shouting from the dining room.

Okay, okay, it's time for y'all to get out!

"Gran Gran, you kicking us out of someone **else's** house?"

"Pepper . . ." Gran Gran nudged Grandpa Pepper.

"Yeah, kids, y'all gotta go," he agreed.

"Go where?" Zola asked.

"Outside."

"And do what?" Herbert asked.

"Walk off that food."

"Walk it off?" Portico asked.

"Well, **you** need to go to your dad's," Gran Gran said. It felt like the trash bag Portico had been lugging around was now a fish bone stuck in his throat. And it was full of . . . not ready.

"I know, I know. But I don't want to go there until I walk my food off, because what if he sees me and says, 'Portico what you doing with all that food on you? I can tell you've been eating green macaroni, and I'm so dis—'"

Go OUTSIDE!

WHAT YOU DO WHEN YOUR GRANDMOTHER TELLS YOU TO GO OUTSIDE AND WALK IT OFF:

1. Go outside.
2. Walk it off.

So that's what Portico, Zola, and Herbert did. They left Zola's apartment, headed down to the stairwell, took a deep breath hoping the weenagers wouldn't be lurking in the in-between, waiting to be rotten, then dashed down flights of stairs, trash bag bumping behind Portico, rushing past all sorts castlemates, from the royals to the spoils, before finally reaching the lobby floor and bolting through the front door, free of the bullies and villains making the stairwell their lair of mean.

And once Portico and his friends were outside it was time to . . .

WALK IT, WALK IT, WALK IT OFF

I'm sure you're confused too, but to walk it off, all you have to do is . . . walk. So Portico and Zola and Herbert started to . . . walk.

Around the building.

Over and over again.

FIRST LAP: They walked their normal pace. Just bopped around the big building like usual. Spoke to the neighbors who were out doing neighborly things.

"Hey, Ms. Wannamaker," Portico said, waving at a woman scrubbing graffiti off the side of the building.

"Hey, y'all!" Ms. Wannamaker replied. "Y'all ain't do this, did you?"

"If we would've done it, it would've been way better than that," Zola murmured.

"Whatchasay, baby?" Ms. Wannamaker asked.

"No, ma'am," Zola said.

And they walked on. And they walked on. And they walked on.

"Hey, Mr. B!" Herbert called out, nodding at Mr. B. He was the neighborhood doctor. No one knew if he was actually a doctor, but he was who everyone in Skylight Gardens called if anything happened to anyone—a broken leg, a sprained ankle, a skinned knee. He was one of those dudes who kept Band-Aids and bandages with him at all times, and even wore one of those heart-hearers around his neck.

"Hey hey, what you kids up to?" Mr. B asked.

"Oh, not much," Portico said. "Just walking it off."

"Ah, well, be careful. And if you can't be careful, come see me and I'll fix you up."

And they walked on. And they walked on.

"Hi, Shaniece," Zola said as they rounded the back of the apartment building. Shaniece worked for Skylight Gardens. Her job was to take care of the bushes and flowers that grew around the building.

"Here come the coolest kids in Skylight Gardens," Shaniece said, cutting and clipping away.

"Shaniece, if we so cool, when you gon' turn us into bushes?" Portico asked. It had been one of his life's goals for the shrubs to be cut into the shape of his face.

"I ain't forget you. But remind me of why I should. Show me what you got."

Portico, Zola, and even Herbert all started striking poses.

Face.

Glamour.

Attitude.

"Okay, okay!" Shaniece said, laughing. "With faces like that, how can I resist!"

And they walked on. Well, it was more of a strut after that.

When they got back to the front door, Portico asked, "Y'all feel like we walked it off?"

Zola poked her belly, macaroni and cheese was still macaroni-ing and cheesing.

"Nope," she said.
"Not yet."

"Another lap?" Herbert asked.

"Another lap," Portico said.

So off they went, again, around the building, passing this person and that person, that person and this person, including Walter and Wendy Walterwendy, a brother and sister who everyone called the cleanagers because they dressed so well. And Rooster, who sped around in her wheelchair. And Hooty, a young man who played the bongos, and Dwayne, who'd come to replace the graffiti Ms. Wannamaker had scrubbed off. He always spray painted the word **"Paradise"** on the wall.

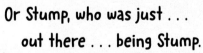

Or Stump, who was just . . . out there . . . being Stump.

After a few more laps, some a slow walk, others a

speed walk, Portico, Zola, and Herbert were approaching the front door. Again.

They were chatting about Episode 105 of *Super Space Warriors*, where Mater and Pater were training Frater and Soror to be good sun protectors by getting them used to the sun's heat.

"Mater said they had to lose their cool," Portico said.

"And then they got in the *Sunjet* and had to get as close to the sun as possible and fly around it over and over and over again until all their cool had been melted off," Zola said. "Frater and Soror got so hot they thought **they** were gonna be . . .

AN EXPLOSION OF GREAT MAGNITUDE!

"But they didn't explode," Herbert said.

"Yeah, 'cause that's not how humans work," Zola reminded them.

"Instead they just got used to the heat!" Herbert said.

"Which brought them one step closer to being better sun protectors," Portico said, now at the building entrance again. "Are we walked off?" he asked, resting the trash bag on the ground for a moment before picking it back up and flinging it back over his shoulder.

"Definitely walked off," both Zola and Herbert said.

But when they opened the front door of the building, standing there, blocking the entrance, was Walnut Head, his noggin taking up most of the space in the doorway.

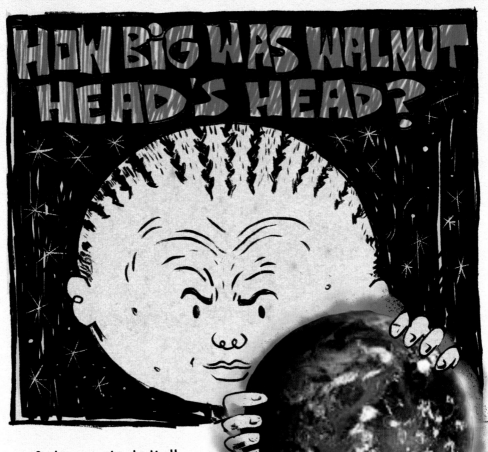

HOW BIG WAS WALNUT HEAD'S HEAD?

As big as a basketball
As big as a classroom globe
As big as a stuffed backpack
As big as Herbert's whole body
As big as the birthday balloons at Zola's party . . .

. . . if a basketball, classroom globe, backpack, Herbert, and a birthday balloon were all the shape of a walnut. And if you don't know what a walnut looks like, well . . . it looks like a brain. Which is funny because that's the one thing Walnut Head didn't have.

176

"Where y'all think y'all going?" Walnut Head asked. "Especially **you** . . . L'il Herby **the Traitor**."

"We going inside. Just finished walking off our lunch," Herbert said.

"Well, y'all can't come in," Walnut Head said, folding his arms.

"Come on, man. We **live** here," Zola said.

"Not no more. We keep dogs and rats outside."

"That's not true," Portico sparked. "I mean, there's a lady on the fourth floor with an apartment full of . . . iguanas!" He set the trash bag down again.

"Also," Herbert added, "**you** got a dog."

It was true. Walnut Head had a dog. Named . . . Rat.

"So what. That don't matter. Y'all ain't coming in unless you come through me."

Portico couldn't stay outside. Not forever. He had to feed A New Name Every Day, and even more importantly, he had to eventually find the courage to go to his father's apartment and give his dad the trash bag full of leftover treasures. And have father-son time. And . . . **SPEND THE NIGHT.**

More, more importantly, Portico had to watch *Super Space Warriors*. The Frater-and-Soror storyline was getting good, and he wanted to see if they'd continue protecting each other as they learned to protect the sun, or if they'd start arguing about everything like Mater and Pater. So Portico's body started rumbling and his organs started discombobulating, and he knew it was time for Stuntboy. But the only stunt he could think of was one he almost never did because it wasn't always as effective as some of the others. It was called, the Stare Well.

HOW TO DO THE STARE WELL

Stare.
That's it. Just stare at someone threatening until they get uncomfortable.

But . . . this could backfire. And if it does backfire, then you'll need to go into a different stunt. A new one Portico had just created called, **the Iguana.**

Here's how you do it: RUN!
Climb the walls if you can!
But again, that's only if the
Stare Well backfires.

Portico closed his eyes to
prepare them for the Stare
Well. And once they were
ready—powered up—he
opened his eyes and . . .
stared.

And stared.

And Walnut Head stared
back.

And Portico stared more.

And Walnut Head stared back, more.

And Portico stared, staringly strong. He'd learned all this
from his parents. He'd watched them stare each other
down whenever they were arguing. He knew how to do this.
He just had to keep holding. No blinking. No backing away.

the Iguana

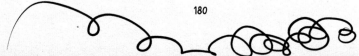

Episode 6
WHEN CHICKENS COME HOME TO CLUCK

Roll credits.
Cue theme music.

Turn it down a bit. A little more.
You know what? How about we go into this episode in
a whisper.

And a one, and a two, and a . . .

WeLLLlllLcoMe to StUNtboyYYy
in-betwEeen Time!!

EMPTY ROOM, BOY OH BOY

Back to the in-between. Portico, Zola, and Herbert started up the stairwell again. When they got to the third-floor landing, Zola turned to Portico.

"Hey, you still going to see your dad?"

"Yeah, of course. Can't wait."

"Well, we right here," Zola said, pointing to the "3" leading out into the third-floor corridor.

"I thought we were gonna finish up at **our** place," Portico said about the apartment up on the eighth floor. The empty one.

"Yeah, but your . . ."

"I'll go see him after that," Portico assured her.

"You could drop that nasty bag off, at least," Herbert said.

"He's always around trash. I don't want to drop more on him and then just leave. We gotta go through it together."

Zola and Herbert followed Portico, step after step, flight after flight, past the people and the people's people, back to the eighth floor to finish their empty-apartment art project. (That's A LOT of steps, especially when you're dragging a big trash bag behind you! Especially since all the food had been walked off.)

The whole time, Portico and Zola tried to find Herbert a hero name.

"Super Jr.?"

"Never."

"Ground Ball?"

"What?"

"Itty Bitty Bull Dog?"

That one, Herbert just growled at.

"What about Empty-Room Boy?" Zola asked as they opened the door to the vacant apartment. Their masterpiece was right where they'd left it. An outburst of art along the walls.

"I like it," Portico said, dropping his bag in the middle of the floor.

"I hate it," Herbert replied. "Why would my name be Empty-Room Boy?"

"Because maybe your superpower is finding empty rooms. I mean, you found this one, right?" Zola said, examining her work in progress. She'd been drawing a lawn chair big enough for the whole world, which was a hard thing to do because she hadn't seen the whole world. Which meant most of her drawing was made-up places, most of which had the word Skylight in them. Skylight Park. Skylight City. Skylight Forest. The Skylight Mountains. And of course, Skylight Gardens.

"What's your superhero name, Zola?" Herbert asked, a little annoyed. *Everyone seems to be asking that question,* Portico thought. *First Gran Gran, now Herbert.*

"Um . . . **Zola**," she said. "Grandpa Pepper named me, and everything he names is special." Herbert had no snappy comeback. Zola was Zola. And that was that.

"Okay, but what's your **superpower**?" Herbert asked. Zola thought for a moment.

"It gotta be meditation'ing," Portico said.

"Anybody can do that," Zola responded.

"What about staying calm?" Portico asked.

"That's part of the mediation," Zola replied.

"So what is it, then? Let me guess, you so cool, your superpower is not needing a superpower?" Herbert rolled his eyes.

Zola walked up to Herbert, looked him in the face, and then . . .

Snatched the marker right out of his hand. Portico's eyes ballooned. Herbert's too.

"I can catch anything," Zola said. "Or **anyone**. So don't ever steal from me again."

COMMERCIAL BREAK: This commercial is brought to you by

WHAT TO DO DURING THE AWKWARD (AND INCREDIBLE) MOMENT ZOLA STANDS UP FOR HERSELF

Be happy she snatched the marker and not your ear. *Ouch!*

Now back to your regularly scheduled program.

Zola stared at Herbert. Stared him down. She almost pulled off the Stare Well, though she wasn't a pro like Portico. But she definitely came close. She handed the marker back to Herbert. Herbert gulped.

Portico broke the tension, refocused the conversation. "Right . . . so . . . uh . . . I mean, just think about it, Herbert. Empty-Room Boy might work, because if your superpower is finding empty rooms like this, we can set up superhero bases all over the place."

"Or, how about Base Boy," Zola followed up.

Herbert thought on it. Back to the drawing board, again. Or, in this case, the drawing walls.

"Fine . . . No Boy," Zola muttered under her breath.

"That's more like it!" Herbert said.

"Oh boy," Zola muttered.

"No, No Boy."

"No-No Boy?" Portico was perplexed.

"Yes," Herbert said.

"Yes No Boy? Or Yes, No-No Boy?"

"Or Maybe So Boy!" Zola yelped, cracking herself up.

"Maybe not," Herbert snarled. "Let's just get back to work. This thing needs some color." He pointed to the art.

They started adding all kinds of colors to each of their

individual pieces, and even started blending **all** the art together. Portico's butterflies flying around Herbert's house. Herbert's house ending up on Zola's lawn chair. Their art was becoming ONE art—a mural, which sounds kinda like mirror, but they aren't the same thing. But they are.

They colored in reds, blues, yellows, and every color they could think of, rainbowing their hearts out.

Until there was a knock at the door.

Which made their hearts knock in their chest.

"Chill," Herbert whispered, trying to play cool. "I locked the door."

They sure were glad Herbert had remembered to do that!

The only problem was, whoever was knocking . . . had a key!

Portico, Zola, and Herbert froze. Watched as the lock slowly turned. From up and down. To sideways. And then the knob started turning.

And then.

And then.

(Cue scary music!)

THE DOOR OPENED! (The door opened?) THE DOOR OPENED!

And standing there . . . standing right there . . . was . . . Soup!

And he looked super. Mad. MAD.

MAD-FACE SOUP (the ingredients)

Eyes: First they were big like quarters. Then small, thin like quarters turned on their sides. Thin, like lasers might shoot out of them.

Nose: Nostrils revving up like an engine.

Mouth: First open, then closed tight. Then, frowning so hard it looked like the bottom half of his face was melting.

Forehead: So wrinkly his wrinkles spelled out **M-A-D**.

Voice: Like a snake speaking English, Soup's voice had become a hiss. Not loud. Just low and slow like air leaking from a tire.

Portico couldn't tell if this was a good thing or a bad thing because he was used to his parents yelling. But then he looked at Herbert, and Herbert didn't seem too much like a fire ant anymore. As a matter of fact, he looked like he wanted to just disappear into the mural they'd made. Become scribbles. Flat lines.

Or a chicken.

"What . . . did . . . you . . . do?" Soup repeated. But Portico and Zola and Herbert stayed quiet.

"What's wrong, L'il Herby?
Cat got your tongue?"

Portico wasn't sure why Soup would ask Herbert something like that. More importantly, he would never want his cat, A New Name Every Day, to get his tongue. Because then he'd be able to lick himself with Portico's tongue, and Portico never wanted to know what cat tasted like, because he had a weird feeling cat tasted a lot like peas and carrots.

"Better answer me," Soup warned.

Herbert stepped forward.

Portico's frets went from zero to high gear in record time, so he stepped forward too. He wasn't sure if he had a stunt for this one. I mean, Soup was a Super, after all. But he knew he couldn't let Herbert stand there alone. Zola felt the same way, so she also stepped up.

"We . . . I . . ." Herbert started. But Soup cut him off because sometimes when grown-ups get mad, they do that.

"How did y'all even get in here?" Soup asked.

"It was open," Herbert explained, his voice mousy.

"The door was open?"

"No, but it was unlocked, so I just . . . came in," Herbert clarified.

"So, let me get this straight. First you were hanging out in the boiler room, which was all kinds of dangerous, and now this. You think you own this building?"

"Well," Portico spoke up. "This is my castle, and—"

"Portico . . ." Soup made a face and Portico stopped talking.

"I'm gonna have to tell your parents about this." Now Soup was looking at Zola. "Yours too, Zola."

Zola dropped her head, looked at the floor, a yoga pose Portico had never seen her do.

"But . . . nobody lives here," Herbert protested.

"But someone will," Soup said. "As a matter of fact, I'm here to meet the new tenant. And now I have to figure out how to explain to them why their new apartment looks like a . . . a . . . circus!"

THINGS THE APARTMENT ACTUALLY LOOKED LIKE:

1. A carnival (more than a circus)

2. The inside of a kaleidoscope

3. The best comic book ever created (maybe called **Stuntboy and Friends**, or **In-Between Time**)

4. A masterpiece

"We'll deal with the consequences later," Soup said. "Right now we need to get all this repainted, pronto." He grabbed Herbert by the arm and marched him out of the apartment to go get white paint to paint over everything. Portico and Zola tried to figure out how they were going to explain this to their parents.

"You think my mother would believe this was an accident?" Portico asked.

"Hmmm. Not sure she's gonna believe we tripped and fell into the room and markers flew out of our hands and hit the walls in this artsy way."

"True, but she's gonna be coming back after meditation'ing, so maybe she'll be so relaxed, she won't be as mad. I mean, after all that toe breathing and pretzeling—"

"I'm just gonna say it was magic," Zola said, catching Portico off guard.

"What?" Portico couldn't believe Zola thought this was a better idea.

"Yep. The markers just came to life and painted what they

wanted to paint. This is the voice of the markers!" Zola said. "I just think this might be better for my mom than to say it was an accident, because she doesn't believe in accidents. But she definitely believes in magic. And these are **magic** markers. So . . . maybe the markers just wanted to be heard." Zola shrugged.

"They wanted to be heard! Yes!" Portico paused, hopeful. "You think that's gonna work?"

"Absolutely not."

Portico plunked to the floor, rested his chin in his hands. "Too bad Herbert is our friend now, because we could've blamed it all on him. I mean, it was **his** idea."

"Yeah. But he **is** our friend now," Zola said, plopping down next to Portico.

"But the weenagers ain't! We could say they did it! Or they forced us." Then Portico shook his head. "But even they don't deserve that."

"Nope, not even the stinky one."

"I guess we just gotta tell the truth," Portico huffed.

"And apologize," said Zola.

Apologize. Ah—pollllll-ohhh-gize. A word like a slow walk toward doom.

And that set Portico's frets on fire all over again. The last time he had to apologize to anyone, it was to Zola for ruining her birthday party with his dance stunts. But he couldn't remember the last time he had to apologize to his **parents**. He tried not to make too many mistakes, especially when they were breaking up. He didn't want to add anything to a tough situation, so he tried super hard to always do things right. Even save the trash his father might want.

"Oh no . . . I gotta . . . apologize?"

Portico's throat started closing. Panic, panic. His heart, racing racing. He stood up, started pacing, pacing. Back and forth across the apartment—Zola couldn't even calm him down—until Herbert Singletary the In-Trouble returned with Soup, carrying cans of white paint and four paintbrushes.

"Okay, everyone get busy," Soup said, popping open the cans, passing out the paintbrushes. His face was still Super mad.

But before the first brush of paint smeared on the wall, there was a **knock at the door.**

This time, even the super froze.

WHAT A MESS-TERPIECE

"Oh no. They're early," Soup groaned, checking his watch. "Well, I guess we have to face the music. Listen y'all, let me do the talking."

Portico was ridiculously happy to hear that Soup would be doing the talking, because he wasn't sure he'd be able to say one single word, **especially** since all his inside-things were now crammed in his throat. Way worse than a fish bone. It was also good news that Soup would be the speaker of the group, because when he opened the door, in came . . .

"Grandpa Pepper?" Zola couldn't believe her eyes. Neither could Portico. He even closed his, then opened them again to make sure his eyes weren't lying to him. They weren't.

"And Gran Gran?" The words felt wrong in Portico's mouth, or maybe his mouth felt wrong around the words, and that was probably because Soup told them he would do all the talking, and here Portico was doing some of the talking, breaking the rules again.

"Porchie, Zola, Air Bear, what y'all doing here?" Grandpa Pepper asked. "Wait, y'all throwing me a surprise birthday party?"

"Today's your birthday?"

"Nope. Not even close, Porchie. But it **will** be in about seven months, so if that's what this is, you nailed the surprise!"

"Grandpa, what **you** doing here?" Zola asked.

"Well, I was gonna surprise **you**, but . . . wait, is this YOUR surprise party? Am I late?"

"Grandpa Pepper, please. What's going on?" This whole conversation was weirding Zola out. Grandpa Pepper could tell she needed answers, so he decided to give her one.

I'M MOVING INTO SKYLIGHT GARDENS!!

"This is my new apartment!" Grandpa Pepper looked around, noticed the magnet on the refrigerator. "At least I thought it was. But looks like someone might already live here."

Surprise! went off in Zola's head but was drowned out by the sound of Soup clearing his throat.

"About that . . ." Soup started. "So . . . my son—"

"Stepson," Herbert nipped.

"My **son**," Soup repeated, "apparently found out that I hadn't locked the door, I guess, so he and his buddies took full advantage and decided to use this empty apartment—**your** empty apartment—as their personal coloring book."

"Wait a minute—" Grandpa Pepper began. But there would be no waiting. Portico lost it.

"It was the iguanas!" he blurted out.

"Portico!" Zola flashed him a look, then squared her shoulders, looked straight at her grandfather. "I'm sorry, Grandpa Pepper. I messed up."

"**We** messed up," Herbert added.

They both turned toward Portico.

"Okay, okay," Portico started over. "I'm sorry I painted this section over here of one butterfly becoming two butterflies and a caterpillar. And I'm also sorry I drew your granddaughter as the beautiful slothicorn she is! **I'm sorrrrry!** And I'm sorry I drew a fire ant on the wall, but"—Portico turned to Soup—"Herbert has a big heart, it's just in his butt!"

Gran Gran gaped as Portico went on and on, her face showing some of the traces of anger that Soup's had when he'd first seen the masterpiece.

"Portico," she said, trying get him to calm down. "Portico stop."

"You mad at me?" he asked, guiltily.

"I'm . . . disappointed in you. You know better."

Disappointed? Oh no! That's the worst possible thing she could've said.

Disappointed?

Disappointed?

Portico thought superhero fast. A verbal stunt, that's what he needed.

"When can we make a new appointment, so disappointment can become dat-appointment, and you can forgive me?"

Gran Gran tried hard not to laugh, because this was a serious moment.

"I forgive you," she said, chewing on her smirk. "But unfortunately it's not my forgiveness you need. Mr. Pepper's the one you need to forgive you."

Portico stepped forward.

"I'm sorry, Mr. Grandpa Pepper," Portico said one more time.

Grandpa Pepper started walking around the room.

He took it all in. Walked from wall to wall almost like he was walking off his . . . shock.

"You know, I'm sorry, too," Grandpa Pepper said at last.

"For what?" Zola asked.

"That y'all were about to paint over this . . .

He'd clearly been watching too much *Super Space Warriors*.

"Huh?" Portico was dazed.

Grandpa Pepper gave the room another look over, spun around as if doing a dance.

"Look, y'all were wrong—**very** wrong to mess up other people's property—but what you made is beautiful, and sometimes that's how life goes." Grandpa Pepper looked at the kids. "I love this place! But it needs a name. I'll call it, The A-heart-ment.

Then he looked at Soup and said "I'll take it."

WHAT MIGHT HAPPEN WHEN YOU GET IN TROUBLE WITH YOUR GRANDPARENTS

1. They might tell you they're disappointed in you, which will make you want to disappear.

2. They might let your cute little face, those teary eyes, those chubby cheeks, that missing tooth, convince them to keep it all a secret.

3. They might tell you they might have to tell your parents, which is way worse than telling you they *will* tell your parents because now you have to wait and see if they actually will tell your parents, and that's like waiting for the worst wish to come true.

COMMERCIAL BREAK: This commercial is brought to you by

WHAT MIGHT HAPPEN WHEN YOU GET IN TROUBLE WITH A PARENT

Anything can happen. But if you're out when you get in trouble, the worst part won't happen until you get home. And when home is right down the hall, like Herbert's is, and your father works in the building you live in, well . . . let's just say playtime is over.

Note: Herbert emptied his pockets and gave every single marker back to Zola. Every. Single. Marker.

COMMERCIAL BREAK: This commercial is brought to you by

SUPERHERO NAMES FOR A GROUNDED FRIEND (named Herbert Singletary)

1. HERBERT SINGLETARY the GROUNDED

2. GROUNDED BOY

3. GROUND BOY

4. TROUBLE MAN

5. DISAPPOINT MAN

6. THE APOLOGIZER

7. HOPEFULLY WE'LL SEE YOU AGAIN BOY

On the next episode of *Super Space Warriors*, Frater and Soror discover the sun port, which is where all the Super Space Warriors' *Sunjets* are kept. You didn't think there was just ONE *Sunjet* did you? No, there are many, many *Sunjets*, but only one that Mater and Pater use most.

So when Frater and Soror, the newest sun protector trainees, find out there are so many *Sunjets* not being used, they decide to pick one way in the back corner of the sun port and act like it's theirs.

They decorate the inside of it, drawing pictures of themselves, and even write their names across the control panel, marking it as their own.

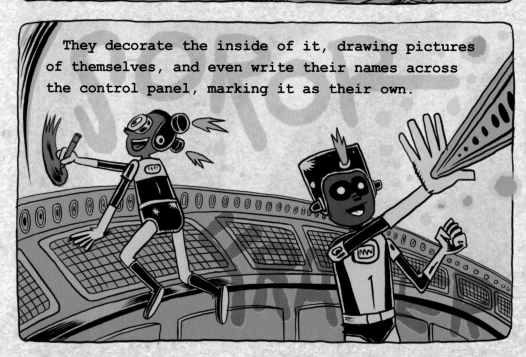

But at some point, playing around in the abandoned spacecraft goes too far, and Frater and Soror start pushing buttons and cause . . .

Will they be able to look Mater and Pater in the face and apologize? Or . . . will they . . .

Find out next time on, *Super Space Warriors*!

♪♫ They have to protect the sun! ♫♪

HEAVY DUTY TRASH BAGS

Seriously, they're good for so many things. You can use them to let things go, or to save things. And in Portico's case, he wishes he could've gotten into the trash bag and saved himself. (Even though his mom and dad might've thrown him out after hearing about this!)

WHY ARE THERE SO MANY COMMERCIAL BREAKS?

1. Commercial breaks are sometimes better than the actual show. Okay . . . maybe not in this case.

2. We just didn't want to embarrass our friends, Portico, Zola, and Herbert. Poor Herbert. He had a long, long walk down the hall. And when he got there, his mother was home. I know how it went—not great—but I just can't tell you those details, even though I know you can keep secrets.

As for Zola, well, even though Grandpa Pepper was happy with the way his new apartment's walls looked (he and Zola even stayed longer so he could do some drawing himself!) he still had to break it to Zola that after they finished making art, he had no choice but to tell her parents what she'd done. He also told her that he'd make sure the punishment wasn't too bad. Drawing is good.

And as far as he was concerned, the whole world did need a giant lawn chair. A place for everyone to just chill out. But doing all this on the walls of an empty apartment she was never supposed to be in was a creative moment gone too far.

And what about our friend Portico? Well, Gran Gran informed him that she would walk him to his downstairs apartment. The new place she stayed in. His father's apartment, 3C.

Now back to your regularly scheduled program.

Episode 7

GOING DOWN!

Roll credits.
Cue theme music.
Let's make it scary.
Slow piano.

That's too slow, now this
whole thing feels romantic!
Jeesh. Let's just start the show.

And a one, and a two, and a . . .
WeLLLlllLcoMe to StUNtboyYYyy in-betwEen TIme

STAIRWELL TO . . .

The journey from the eighth floor to the third floor was a long one, mainly because Gran Gran took each step as if she was walking on quicksand. As if the step would collapse under her feet. It was a slow process. This was hard for Portico because he'd been so used to running and jumping down them. He hadn't been doing too much of that today because of the trash bag he'd been lugging around. But also because so many people were crowded onto the stairs, moving up, moving down. Not to mention, some were just standing in the way, like screenagers, who don't really move anywhere. They just stand still and stare at their phones while everyone screams at them to get out the way. Or the leanagers, who just lean against the railing, making it hard for ladies Gran Gran's age to get by.

Portico would normally say "'Scuse me," because he was taught manners by his parents, and especially by his grandmother. But turns out she didn't really believe in those same manners for herself, and she went with a more direct approach.

Gran Gran's voice was a bark, but still Gran Gran-y. Still sweet, like a cat's meow.

And guess what? People moved. Everyone. The old heads like Mr. Mister, and Mr. Chico, and even Mama Gloria. Even the screenagers. And the leanagers. Everybody respected Gran Gran, even all the betweenagers.

Most of all, Portico.

Gran Gran tried giving Portico a before-punishment pep talk.

"Now, I'm gonna be here, so your father's not gonna be too hard on you. Do you want to tell him, or should I?"

"Can't we keep it a secret?" Portico begged.

"Oh, grandson," Gran Gran said, her face softening. "I wish I could. But you know my rule. I can only cover for you once. And, honestly, I've been covering for you all day. We have to tell him. I don't feel good about it, but . . . one of us has to."

Portico understood, but he still had some bargain in him.

"Okay, well, I think you—" But before Portico finished his sentence, Gran Gran cut him off.

"You'll tell him. I know you're brave enough to own up to your mistakes, right?"

Portico sulked and started dragging his feet while also dragging his bag, step after step.

"Yes, ma'am. I just don't know **why** I have to tell him, though. Especially since Mr. Grandpa Pepper loves it. It was basically a stunt that kept him from having to decorate his walls by himself!" Portico tried to sound convincing.

"Oh, **really?** So what you call that stunt?" Portico was caught off guard and before he could come up with anything, Gran Gran barreled on. "I got an idea for a good name for that **stunt**. The **perfect** name. How about you call it, **Lying to My Father**. Got a nice ring to it, right?" She eased down onto the fifth floor landing. Two more flights to go before the **uh-oh**.

Portico thought about it and realized he didn't like that stunt name, mainly because it **was** perfect. And that made him sad. Because lying to his father wasn't a stunt. Not like his regular ones. Not like the ones he'd used to try to save his parents from themselves. Or the ones he'd used to save Zola 216 days before on the first day of school, even though now he knows she can save herself. Or the ones he'd been using all day to save Herbert from the weenagers.

"Sound good?" Gran Gran asked.

"No ma'am," Portico said. And just then, Gran Gran's phone rang.

She answered, and there, on a video call, was Portico's mother.

"Oh hey, Sasha. How's your retreat going?" Gran Gran asked.

"It's been wonderful. I feel like I'm coming back to myself," Portico's mother said, her voice soft, peaceful.

"Well, I'm not sure what that means but it sure sounds nice."

"Did Portico make it to his dad's apartment?"

Portico's eyes almost jumped out of his face. Gran Gran nudged him.

"I'm here, Ma." Portico's voice went shaky as Gran Gran handed him the phone.

"Hey. You okay?"

"Yeah, I'm good. Have you learned to breathe through your toes yet?"

"I'm working on it. But why aren't you at your dad's? What have you been doing all day?" his mother double asked.

Portico looked at his grandmother.

"Think of it as practice for the big show," Gran Gran whispered.

Portico told his mother what had happened. About how Herbert had found an empty apartment, and how they'd gone in and expressed themselves all over the walls.

"You mean you drew all over **someone else's walls?** You've never even drawn on the walls in our house!

And you better not do that at your father's, either. Speaking of, does your father know about all this? Where is that man?"

"I'm going there now." He and Gran Gran were one floor away.

"You never went?!"

"No." Portico then explained all about the elevator, and how he'd gotten distracted and how the stairwell had been a weird place.

"Portico . . . you better get your narrow behind down there right now." And before any other veins popped out of his mother's forehead, Zola's mother popped onto the screen. She tried calming Portico's mom down. Breathing exercises.

Breathe in. Breathe out.

Breathe in. SCREAM out!

THINGS MOTHERS SAY WHEN THEY FIND OUT YOU DID SOMETHING YOU HAD NO BUSINESS DOING

Wait. First . . .

THINGS YOU HAD NO BUSINESS DOING

1. Those things you did.

Now, back to THINGS MOTHERS SAY WHEN THEY FIND OUT YOU DID SOMETHING YOU HAD NO BUSINESS DOING

1. You had no business doing that!

2. What were you thinking?!

3. Are you kidding? Is this a joke?

4. But you know better!

5. Go to your room!

6. I'm so disappointed!

There's that word again. Disappointed. It felt like a
pointy word, a word that pricked the ear, and the throat, and
the eyes, and the belly. A word similar to divorce. And when
his mother finally finished strong-talking him, he realized
the weenagers were all gathered right by the third floor
door, looking at him, laughing their ugly heads off.

"Uh-oh, is Port-a-Potty in trouble?" Piano growled. Piano flashed a smile, every other tooth missing, making it less of a smile, and more of s i e. "Your mommy gonna ground you? She gon' send you to your room without din-din? No dessert tonight? No bedtime stories? Your mommy gonna put you in timeout? Let me guess, she told you she was disappointed in you, right?" Piano trolled on and on. And Portico tried to hold in his feelings. Tried to control the frets, which had started a bunch of steps before this point. Frets that bloomed up on the eighth floor, and grew with each flight of stairs, and grew more when his mother called, and grew even more as he and Gran Gran approached the third floor door. The doorway that would lead them to apartment 3C, where his father would be waiting for him.

He tried to think of what Mater or Pater or Frater or Soror would do, but couldn't.

He couldn't think of a single stunt.

Fortunately, he wouldn't have to. Because . . .

GRAN GRAN'S GOT STUNTS TOO

Here are a few:

1. The Granny Growl: It's a not a sound. It's a tone in the back of the throat. One that reminds you that you're close to . . . something you don't want to be close to. It's a warning that don't even sound like a warning.
2. The Help Me Honey: This is when, in the middle of a tough situation, grandmothers ask for help. With something high on a shelf. Or to pick something up off the floor. Or to open the door. Melts tough guys instantly.
3. The Big Mama Memory: This is when grandmothers bring up embarrassing old stuff you don't even remember. But they do. They remember it all. Every detail.

And The Big Mama Memory is what Gran Gran went with as Piano kept teasing Portico.

"Who that making all that fuss? Percy, is that you? That can't be you talking like that," Gran Gran said. Immediately all the other weenagers started snickering at . . . **Percy.**

"Yes ma'am, it's me," Piano said, sheepishly.

"The same Percy who's mother had to bring him to the hospital to see me every other month because you could only sleep if you rocked back and forth, knocking your head against your bedpost until you passed out? Always had a big ol' knot on your forehead."

"Uh . . . I . . . I don't remember that," Piano said, glancing behind at his friends. "I don't remember that at all."

"I bet you don't, banging your head like that your whole childhood. It's a wonder you can remember anything!" Gran Gran reached out for

BABY PERCY

Piano's head. "Matter fact, come here and let me look at your noggin to see if there's any permanent damage."

But Piano couldn't take any more embarrassment and decided to make a run for it. And the other weenagers were right behind him.

MAD DAD

When Portico and Gran Gran arrived at apartment 3C, Gran Gran stuck her key into the keyhole, then turned to Portico.

"Ready?"

Portico nodded.

"You can do this. It's gonna be okay," she said.

Portico took a deep breath, nodded again. His grandmother had never lied to him, and he knew she wouldn't, but it was hard to feel like this was going to be okay.

Gran Gran turned the key, then turned the knob, then pushed the door open. And there, sitting on the couch, was Portico's father. He jumped to his feet.

MY SON HAS FINALLY ARRIVED!

he exclaimed as if he was, in fact, announcing the prince of the castle.

"Hi, Dad." Portico heaved the bag of trash he'd been carrying everywhere—up the stairs, down the stairs, into Herbert's apartment, and Zola's apartment, and the empty apartment— and and and . . . set it down in the middle of the floor.

Portico's father hugged him. Squeezed him tight. Lifted him off the ground.

"Marvin, Portico has something he wants to tell you," Gran Gran said, all kinds of serious.

Portico's father set Portico back down. Then sat back down.

"What's going on?" he asked. "And what's in that bag?"

Portico thought this was the **perfect** moment to talk about exactly what **was** in the bag . . . father-son time, feeding the trash monster, looking through old stuff from old times. But Gran Gran was right there to keep him on task.

"He'll tell you about that after he tells you about what happened up on the eighth floor."

"Gran Gran," Portico groaned.

"What? Just trying to help," she assured him as she left the room.

"On the eighth floor?" Portico's father turned the TV off.

Portico stood in front of his dad, his insides all mismatched, his lungs in his stomach, his belly coughing.

"Um . . . so . . . " Portico tried to find the words. Well, actually that's not true. All the words were right there in the front of his mind, but he was trying to . . . **not** find them. "It . . . it all started with Herbert telling us about this . . . um . . . this . . . apartment." Portico's eyes began to water.

"Uh-huh."

"Up there."

"Uh-huh."

"That was empty."

"Okaaaaaaaay."

"And . . . unlocked." And from there, Portico spilled the rest of the beans.

Portico's father looked at Portico like he had three heads. Or . . . twelve toes.

"But why would you draw all over the walls?" he said at last.

Portico shrugged.

"That's not a good enough answer." Portico's father squared his jaw. "Try again."

"I don't know," Portico whimpered, his eyes now swimming.

"I think . . . it just felt so cool to be with my friends, just hanging out somewhere that felt . . . like . . . ours."

"But, Portico, that place wasn't yours."

"I know. But . . . but . . . I guess the togetherness—"

"**Togetherness** made you lose your **mind**?!" Portico's father was trying not to raise his voice, and failing.

"No . . . it . . . it . . . **re**-minded me." The words vibrated in Portico's throat.

"Reminded you?"

"Yeah, reminded me of what it meant to be in one place with . . . your people." His eyes were now practically drowning. His voice went almost voiceless. "Like how our old apartment used to feel . . . before . . ." The words that were supposed to complete that sentence came out as tears instead.

Portico's father softened his tone. "So that's what this is about?"

Portico looked down, wiped his tears. His father tilted his chin, lifted his face. Eye to eye.

"But, son, you have to also understand that that's still not a good enough reason to go around drawing all over other people's walls."

"I know."

"Meanwhile, I'm down here waiting on you. I'm guessing that's why you're so late, right?"

"Sorta. Yeah." Portico sniffled. He explained that the real reason he was late was because, even though he was excited to spend the night,

HE WAS ALSO SCARED TO.

Because it meant the in-between time was a forever thing. His father understood. And Instead of trying to convince Portico it would all be fine, he just listened. And listened. And listened, as Portico flooded him with details about the broken elevator, the iguanas, the fish bone, and walking it off. About Zola's superpower, and the weenagers, and even the look on Gran Gran's face when she caught him on the eighth floor.

By the time Portico had gotten it all out, his father's face had gone from frown to . . . not-quite-smile, but not-frown-anymore. He was still mad, but it was hard not to chuckle at all the hijinks. But still, he had to be a dad.

"I hate to do this, but you know I gotta tell your mother."

"She already knows," Gran Gran said, coming from her room dressed in her night clothes.

Portico's father turned to Gran Gran. "Here's what I wanna know, Ma. What were you doing on the eighth floor?"

"I told you, I had to meet a friend."

"What friend?"

"None of your business," Gran Gran stung.

"His name is Mr. Grandpa Pepper," Portico said. "He's Zola's grandfather, wears nail polish and cool jewelry."

"He's moving into that apartment," Gran Gran added.

"Oh yeah? And how did he feel about y'all ruining his walls?"

"He **loved** it!"

"He **loved** it?" Portico's father glanced at Gran Gran.
She nodded.

"He loved it."

PUNISHMENT

Even though Portico had told his mother and father the
truth, his father still had to punish him. It's just what
parents do. He ordered pizza, and he and Portico talked about
his trip to Las Vegas with Gran Gran. About how Gran Gran
had won a few dollars and he'd lost a few.

"But I still had a good time," he said, which Portico didn't
understand because he'd never had a good time losing
anything. Not a game. Not a tooth. Not a friend. Not a . . .

family. But his father had a way of always seeing the good in things. Portico figured that must've been from all those years working as a trash man.

Obviously, pizza and conversation ain't punishment, but Portico's father made it clear that punishment would come after the pizza. After all the talking.

"When you finish that slice, you're going to bed," he said as Portico nibbled on his last piece of crust. "And tomorrow we're doing litter pickup around the building, and also sweeping the entire stairwell, top to bottom. Clean the in-between."

Portico didn't protest. He knew there had to be some kind of consequence. He'd learned that from when he got into a tussle with Herbert at the block party a few weeks before.

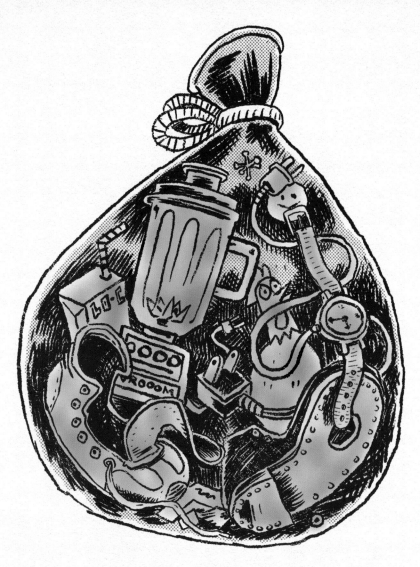

His father pointed to Portico's bag. "Let's be sure to throw that trash out too."

"That's not trash!" Portico piped up. "I mean, it is, but it . . . might not be." Portico set the crust down on his plate, the porcelain painted by the grease. "Ma put a bunch of leftover stuff in here, and I didn't want to throw it out until I went through it with you. Just in case."

THE "JUST IN CASE" THINGS FOUND IN THE BAG
1. A pair of old sneakers, holes in the soles.
2. An old watch. No tick. No tock.
3. A broken blender.
4. An old phone charger.
5. A bunch of other stuff

They rummaged through most of it, Portico marveling at each thing as if he was pulling treasure from a chest, when his father decided that enough was enough.

"Hey, I really appreciate you saving all this for me, especially since you had to keep it safe all day. It had to be pretty heavy."

"You're welcome. It wasn't too bad." Portico flexed his muscles. "Plus, I knew you'd want it."

His father grinned, but only for a second. Half a second.

"Son, I don't know how to tell

you this, but . . . there's just nothing here worth holding on to," he said.

"What you mean? What about this water bottle? Or this comb? Or this bowl. I know it got a crack in it, but a crack don't mean it's ruined," Portico pleaded. "Or what about these batteries? You don't want to just leave batteries not battery-ing. They gotta charge something up, because if they don't, all that energy just builds and builds and can cause . . . AN EXPLOSION OF GREAT MAGNITUDE!"

Portico's father smirked, took the batteries and the comb and everything else and started putting them all back in the bag. He gathered the neck of it, twisted it shut. Then he set the bag by the front door before coming back over to Portico.

"Listen, these things have had their time," he said, now walking Portico down the hall to his room. His **new** room. His **not-sure-he-wanted-a-room-here** room. "And if we can let them go, which we should, because they just don't work anymore . . ." He paused, cleared the bush he'd been beating around from his throat, and continued. "Me and your mom . . . we, um . . . we just don't work anymore. But, that's okay. That's okay. Because now there's space for the new. New memories. A new place. New stuff."

"New stuff?" Portico wasn't sure he liked the sound of that. So far all the "new" stuff had been more like "no" stuff.

Portico's father opened the bedroom door, and on Portico's bed, glowing like some kind of special space rock, were . . .

SUPER SPACE WARRIOR BEDSHEETS!

Portico's eyes went wide.

"Like 'em?" his father asked.

Portico nodded, he couldn't take his eyes off them. Mater. Pater. The *Sunjet*. There was even a place for the sun.

Portico's father kissed him on the top of his head and told him the list of chores would be stuck to the refrigerator in the morning. And as he closed the door to Portico's new bedroom, the faint **ding!** of the elevator coming from the other side of the wall, Portico noticed something on the table beside his bed. A key! Portico had never had a key before, and knew (because . . . **parents**) there would be a conversation about it in the morning where his father would use big confusing words like "responsibility," which really just means, **don't lose this**. And Portico was cool with that. Because 1. It had a shoestring connected to it to go around his neck (so he wouldn't lose it). And 2. **He. Had. A. Key!** He would guard it with his life and couldn't wait to develop new stunts like **Unlock the Door Before Peeing On Yourself**. And, of course, others. But . . . mainly that one.

Oh, and there was something else about the key: a small

keychain was attached to it. Because, seriously, what's a key without one?

And that keychain was yellow and red and rubber.

And from Las Vegas.

Seven-Seven-Seven.

EPISODE 8: A BOY CAN DREAM

Roll credits.
Cue theme music.

Bring in the
puppeteers!
And a one,
and a two,
and . . .

WellLLllllcoMe to
StUNtboyYYyy in-betwEen
TIme!

INTRODUCING THE SON AND ONLY

This is Portico Reeves. He's a best best friend to Zola (for 216 days) and also now to Herbert Singletary (for 1 day). And after a long day of Explosions of Great Magnitude, he has fallen asleep. Again. This time, in a different bed. In a different apartment. With a different parent.

All still his.

He's a snorer. Or as he calls it, he has villain repellent in his nose.

Oh, and he's also a dreamer.

DOWNSY-UPPSY

In tonight's dream, Portico was on the fourth floor outside
his old apartment, but, again, the door was bolted shut.
While trying to force it open anyway, he heard his father
calling him. He ran downstairs, only to still be on the fourth
floor. Then he heard his mother calling him, so he ran back
upstairs, two flights, to what should've been the fifth floor.
But wasn't. He was still on the fourth floor.

He heard both parents, again, calling his name, louder
and louder.

PORTICO!
PORTICO!
PORTICO!

And as Portico moved back down the hallway, he realized their voices were coming from apartment 4D.

But now the door was no longer bolted.

Portico pulled it open, and there his parents were, standing in the middle of an empty apartment. No furniture, a single magnet on the refrigerator, and an iguana crawling slowly across the counter.

His mother pointed at the walls, which happened to be covered in drawings. The same drawings Portico had drawn earlier. Of the butterflies and the caterpillar. Portico stood between his parents staring at the piece in front of him.

Then Portico pulled
markers from his pockets.
Three to be exact.

He gave one to his
mother.

And one to
his father.

Episode 9

AND ALSO

This is Stuntboy. Formerly known as the greatest superhero you've never ever heard of. Now he's one-third of the superhero group, Stuntboy, Zola, and . . . Air Bear.

Who **knows** what they'll get into next.

And does Gran Gran know her grandson's a superhero?
If so, has she **always** known?

Matter fact, where is Gran Gran? She was just here!

To be continued . . .

You asked for them, you got 'em—more of
Raul's sketches . . . I mean, practice stunts. . . .

ZWIPT!

JASON REYNOLDS is a #1 *New York Times* bestselling author, a Newbery and Printz Award honoree, a two-time National Book Award finalist, a Kirkus Prize winner, a two-time Walter Dean Myers Award winner, and the recipient of multiple Coretta Scott King Honors. He was also the 2020–2022 National Ambassador for Young People's Literature. Most recently, he was named the 2023 Margaret A. Edwards Award winner. His many books include *All American Boys* (cowritten with Brendan Kiely); *When I Was the Greatest*; *As Brave As You*; the Track series (*Ghost, Patina, Sunny,* and *Lu*); *Look Both Ways*; *Stuntboy, in the Meantime*; *Ain't Burned All the Bright* (a Caldecott Honor book); and *Long Way Down*. He lives in Washington, DC. You can find his ramblings at JasonWritesBooks.com.

RAÚL THE THIRD is the four-time Pura Belpré Award-winning author-illustrator of *Lowriders to the Center of the Earth*, *¡Vamos! Let's Go Eat*, *¡Vamos! Let's Go to the Market*, and *¡Vamos! Let's Cross the Bridge*, which was also named a New York Times Best Illustrated Book of the Year. He's also the illustrator of the *New York Times* bestselling *Stuntboy, in the Meantime*. He lives in Medford, MA, with his wife and collaborator, Elaine Bay, and their son, Raúl the Fourth. Visit him at RaultheThird.com.

Acknowledgments

JASON:
First and foremost, I want to thank Raúl because these stories are made infinitely better by your vision. The same has to be said for Caitlyn Dlouhy. You're an amazing conductor of these strange symphonies. Thank you to Elena Giovinazzo, whose children I could've dedicated this book to (got 'em on the next one!) And lastly, to all the Stuntkids out there who don't let frets get in the way of fun!

RAÚL:
I'd like to thank my art director, Michael McCartney, for keeping me on track as I slowly chipped away at the hundreds of drawings that I needed to produce. Thanks as well to Caitlyn Dlouhy and Jason Reynolds, it's inspiring to work with you both. And lastly, thanks to Portico Reeves for drawing with a yellow marker.